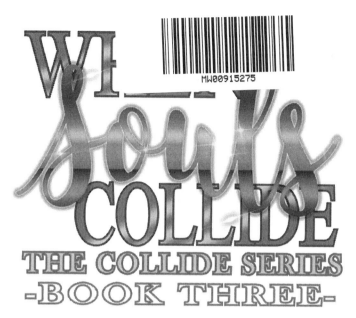

WHEN Souls COLLIDE

THE COLLIDE SERIES

-BOOK THREE-

A Trilogy by Millie Belizaire

MillieBelizaire.com

Edited by **Christina D.**
Cover Designed by **Millie Belizaire**
eBook Formatting by **Millie Belizaire**

Table of Contents

Author's Note

Thank you for reading.

And a special thanks to the fantastic group of ladies I've met while finishing up this series. Your kind words and support have meant the world to me!

Don't forget to leave a review (:

Chapter One

KAIN

Anger is a complexed set of emotions.

To the best of my knowledge, there had only ever been two types of anger. The kind of anger you feel towards a friend or peer who disappoints you—this kind is fleeting and harmless. The kind of anger that makes you violent—this kind is self-explanatory. It was my girlfriend Lauren Caplan's father, the summer of 2016, who showed me that there was a third type of anger.

The kind of anger that makes you calm. This is the kind of anger that makes you calculate. It thrusts you five steps ahead of the situation, and really makes you think before you react. This must be the kind of anger that makes people spend months plotting a murder instead of just outright doing it.

He shot her.

Accidentally or not, he fucking *shot* her, his own daughter. Lauren was lying in a hospital bed somewhere, breathing through a machine, not because of my father, but because of her own.

The truth of the matter was, Silas deserved to be in prison for any one of his crimes over the last thirty plus years. But today, Silas, ironic as can be, was behind bars for the one thing he actually did not do. And me—I was being strong-armed into taking the witness stand for a two-year investigation that had nothing to do with Lauren, in order to save her life. Her life that her own father had put on the line.

I was calm.

I was so angry that I was calm.

Pulling into the parking lot of the Miami-Dade courthouse, I was met with a swarm of photographers. The walk to the building was a trying one. But the flashing of cameras accompanied by the shouting of questions meant to anger me rolled off my shoulders.

"Is it true you helped your father capture and kill Joshua Caplan's daughter?"

"Kain, are you here to sell your father out in order to clear your own name after what happened to Lauren Caplan?"

"Did you convince Lauren to run away from home?"

"Are you taking the stand against your father today in an effort to win Lauren back?"

"What do you say to the allegations Luxana Petit has lodged against you to the press?"

Every single one of their questions went ignored, as I offered no reaction to the inflammatory statements. Climbing the steps up to the main entrance was almost done in a haze. I could hear the reporters on either side of my face trying their hardest to incite me, but at the same time, I couldn't hear them at all. The energy it would take to let them get the best of me—I was saving that.

Upon passing through the security check-in in the courthouse's main lobby, it was seconds before I was shuffled into a private back room. She said her name was Violet—or Veronica—something with a V. I was only half listening to her briefing when I interrupted.

"Caplan." She stopped talking. "Where is he?"

"I just said that he was about to begin his opening arguments. He's going to address the jury, and when you're needed, you'll be called in." To the skeptical crease forming between my brows, she explained even further. "Mr. Caplan thought it would be best if you didn't sit in on the hearing until it was time for you to testify. Your father can be pretty intimidating and he didn't want non-verbal cues from him to change your mind, or sway your answers."

For two years, Joshua Caplan had been extensively investigating Silas' involvement in a New Year's multi-murder that resulted in the deaths of some men who were known to be longtime enemies. Did Silas do it? Of course he did. Did I have proof? Sure. Was I going to help Joshua Caplan take him down for it?

Fuck that.

The room I was in was presumably behind the trial room the case was being tried in. If I focused hard enough, I could almost make out the sounds of Lauren's father presenting monologues and calling up expert witnesses who could analyze the crime scene and weapons ballistics. I was being watched like a criminal in this room, the court aide hardly seemed to be blinking as she stared suspiciously in my direction.

How do you best a man like Joshua Caplan?

An earlier version of myself would learn what I know now, and immediately start cracking my knuckles. But that wasn't thinking smart. Knowing the kind of man Joshua Caplan was, he'd live for that kind of spectacle. No, to best a man like Joshua Caplan, I would need to hit him where it hurts. And that, I had already gathered, was not going to be a physical blow.

"Mr. Montgomery, they're ready for you now."

The trial room was made of wood on every surface, polished browns reflecting back at me like an old fashioned scene straight out of those 90s TV dramas. Stepping into the room created a hush among the invited spectators and jury. Caplan waited until I was seated at the raised, closed in the seat beside the judge. My eyes scanned my surroundings, landing on the name plate of a staunch Cuban judge. *Rodrigo Lopez*, it read, positioned in front of the poker faced, middle aged man.

Caplan introduced me to the jury, careful to lay emphasis on my last name and then let them know I was Silas' only son. My eyes cut away from Judge Lopez's nameplate and for the first time since entering the room, I looked at my father. It appeared as though they hadn't let him change out of his prison uniform, the jumpsuit shining bright orange among the grays and blacks worn by just about everyone else.

For me, Silas saved the most hateful of glares. At least, what he could muster convincingly enough to be seen as hate. I knew my father well. He would never hate me. Was he angry I was testifying? Hell fucking yes. But one look at him and I knew that, more than anything, my being here hurt him more. This was betrayal in the worst way.

Caplan nodded for his bailiff to bring and hold out a hardcover, black bible out in front of me. I knew damn well that I had no intention of telling the truth this morning. The Bible was held out in front of me, and what little left of me that still believed in God felt certain that I would be forgiven for what I was about to do. With my hand on the Holy Book, looking away from Silas, I pledged the oath.

"I, Kain Tariq Montgomery, swear that the evidence that I shall give, shall be the truth, the whole truth and nothing but the truth, so help me God."

Joshua Caplan cleared his throat, walking up to my booth. He eyed me with a heightened level of caution, which bothered me. Who was the real monster here? It wasn't like I was willing to stoop so low as to threaten to kill my own daughter in the name of winning a case. And for what? Is the honor even worth it if that's how low you have to go to get it?

I kept my expression neutral, understanding that I was going to have to do this believably, and if I lied on the stand with a trace of anger on my face, out went my credibility.

"Mr. Montgomery," Caplan began his questioning, keeping eye contact as he paced about the room. "Would you agree with the statement that your father, Silas Montgomery, is a dangerous man?"

"Dangerous?" I feigned ignorance, keeping my eyes on Caplan long enough to see his brows dip at the unexpected response. "Dangerous seems a bit dramatic."

"What would you call it then?"

"Dad is..." I pretended to think about it, shaking my head and ultimately saying, "I admit that he can be somewhat of a hardass, but I'd wager to say most dads are."

"A hardass?"

I shrugged.

"Dad can be... he can be strict. You know the deal—do your homework, go to college, get a good job." Silas never encouraged me to do any of that shit.

"Mr. Montgomery, you do realize your father is on trial for three counts of murder, correct?"

"I realize those are the charges, yeah." I nodded casually. "But you asked me if I thought he was dangerous. Short answer—no."

Caplan's eyebrow twitched very slightly, the only sign of his discomfort. His star witness was not playing ball. As if the room had suddenly grown warmer, he pulled at the collar of his white dress shirt.

"Mr. Montgomery, you say your father encouraged you to get a good job. Isn't that a little hard to believe considering he transferred over a billion dollars' worth of his assets over to you three years ago, when you turned eighteen?"

"That's more of an opinion, if you ask me," I answered back.

"Did he or did he not transfer his assets?"

"He did."

"Ladies and gentleman of the jury, let the record show that the investigation into these murders coincides with Silas Montgomery's decision to transfer all of his assets to his young son. Over a billion dollars handed over to one child. Was that insurance just in case he lost this case? Was Silas trying to make sure his assets weren't frozen in the event that he was put away?

I shook my head, matching his theatrics when I replied, "Ladies and gentleman of the jury, let the record show my father was battlin' with complications brought on by his rising blood pressure three years ago. There are medical records to prove it. Yes, transferring his assets to me was insurance, but only because he felt like he didn't have much time left."

I was lying effortlessly.

"Yes or no—are you aware that the investigation into your father had begun around that time as well?"

"He's a black billionaire. Someone is always investigating him."

Caplan's patience was wearing thin. He was getting nothing useful out of me. I could see him very poorly trying to keep his temper in check. In his seat, Silas leaned forward like a person watching a movie that just got good. Caplan cleared his throat, walking closer to my podium for his next question.

"What do you say to accusations that your father uses his clubs to launder drug and prostitution money?"

"You said it yourself. He doesn't own them; I do. So is this relevant?"

Caplan lost some of his nerve and shot me the question, "Do you use your clubs to launder drug and prostitution money?"

"Well first, I'm not on trial so you're gettin' off topic. And second, I just think it's real telling how a black man in America can't make a large amount of money without someone thinking there's criminal activity just around the corner."

"It's pretty well known around this town that your family is mixed up in some pretty criminal offenses."

"Objection," I intercepted. "That's speculation."

"Sustained," the judge beside me agreed.

I cut my eyes to Silas' table, annoyed that his own team of lawyers had not made a single objection to Caplan's flawed ass questioning. Caplan had asked me at least three questions so far that would've sustained an objection. *Where the fuck did Silas get these lawyers?*

"So you stand by the claim that your father is harmless?" Caplan moved to confirm.

I nodded. "Pretty much."

"So answer me this," Caplan started. "Where was your father on July 31st, between the hours of three and five?"

My eyes narrowed. That was the night Lauren was shot. *This piece of shit is not about to go there.*

Caplan repeated the question, getting very off topic. "Where was your father on July 31st, between the hours of three and five?"

"He was in Memphis."

"Where were you?"

"Objection," I replied. "This has no relevance."

Judge Lopez slammed his mallet once. "Overruled."

"Answer the question, Kain. I'm gonna bring it all back to the topic at hand, don't worry." Caplan crossed his arms, keeping his eyes on mine. "Where were you?"

"I was leaving a club after my birthday."

"With who?"

"You already know who."

"The jury doesn't," Caplan retorted, restating the question. "Who were you with?"

"My girlfriend."

"What. Is. Her. Name?"

He was trying to catch me in a vulnerable spot in order to trip me up. The name almost passed painfully through my throat. "Lauren."

"Lauren *what*?"

"You know her fuckin' last name." I refused to bend. "She's your daughter."

Nobody in the courtroom was surprised. Evidently they had all been tuned in to the news. Caplan went on to give a short monologue.

"Ladies and gentleman of the jury, on July 31st, my *daughter*, Lauren Alyssa Caplan, going through a bit of a rebellious phase, was out with the defendant's son. That night, a lone gunman happens upon them and shoots my daughter. The defendant's son was left unharmed. Isn't that convenient?"

Caplan was painting an ugly picture, made worse by the fact that he knew more than anyone exactly what happened that night. He already knew who the "lone" gunman was. And just when I thought it couldn't get any worse, a picture of Lauren in her hospital bed was put up on a screen for the whole courthouse to see. I swallowed, feeling a lump forming in my throat.

He continued to address the jury. "Now, Lauren's shooting is a separate incident, and not what the defendant is on trial for, but let the records show that Lauren's best friend has come forward and attested to the media that Lauren told her in April that Silas Montgomery wanted her dead as an attack on me, an attempt to sabotage *this* case. Why would an innocent man go to such lengths? Kain Montgomery, allegedly, told Lauren to not contact authorities because he could - quote - keep her safe himself. A few months later, after running away from home to be with him, she was shot in a parking lot. What do you say to that, Kain?"

I shook my head at the nerve. Anger—the violent kind—was brewing from within me. "She didn't run away from home. You kicked her out and she had nowhere else to go."

"So everything else I said was true?"

I couldn't lie about this one. It would implicate me later if Lauren woke up and decided to talk. She had the text messages to prove it. Hell, she had a whole phone that I paid the bill for somewhere. She could hang us all out to dry the moment she woke up. And after practically getting shot in the chest, who would blame her?

"I plead the fifth." Pleading the fifth amendment on the stand never looks good. Caplan smiled, taking that as a win.

"Why would Silas Montgomery want to kill my daughter?"

"If that's even true—that's a question for Silas Montgomery," I replied.

"So you're saying that's not true??"

I nodded.

"So what were you protecting her from, Kain?"

I lied, "I wasn't protecting her from anything."

"Clearly," Caplan stated, gesturing toward the photo of Lauren in her hospital bed displayed. That one hit me right where it hurt. I flinched, prompting him to come to the realization, "You love her, don't you?"

"This isn't relevant."

"It's a simple yes or no question."

"It's a simple yes or no question that isn't relevant."

My combativeness set something off within the man facing me.

"Do you *really* think you love her?" Caplan shouted. He was skeptical and very clearly losing his temper. The jury whispered among themselves, casting worried looks to the back of Caplan's head. I glanced at Silas' lawyer, willing him to intercept this courtroom violation. Silas held his counsel down, wanting Caplan to continue on the tirade he was on. I understood the motive.

As Caplan stayed off topic, talking about Lauren, who was not what this case was about, he was essentially throwing away his own credibility. He looked unhinged, incompetent, too emotional. This had all the trappings of a mistrial.

Caplan was going to make himself look like a raving dumbass, using tax payer money to simply drill into a boyfriend he didn't approve of. It appeared as though everyone in the room could see Caplan fucking up, except for Caplan himself. Silas' lawyers did not interrupt Caplan's unprofessionalism—a smart move for them, absolute torture for me.

Silas was going to win this case through a technicality. And all he needed to do was let Caplan keep talking about Lauren.

"And so… how do you…. How do claim that you love someone, and then ultimately set them up for murder?" What the fuck was he accusing me of? No way… Was he really gonna act like I had something to do with the hit he carried out? Joshua Caplan wasn't human. "Did you help your father set Lauren up?" He was reaching record levels of low. "Riddle me this… after she was shot, why did you bother calling the ambulance at all? Don't you think you ruined your father's plan?"

I hit back. "Objection. Inflammatory."

If Silas' lawyers weren't going to do anything about this highly unprofessional questioning, I was going to fucking do it myself.

"Why do you go to the hospital as often as you do? You think we don't know you have some sort of agreement with the night staff?"

"Objection. Relevance."

"Do you *really* think that you love her?"

"Objection. Relevance."

"Lauren is in the hospital because of you, Kain. She's one foot in the grave, and it's your fault!" He was unstable. Because I knew the truth about how Lauren had come to have one foot in the grave, I was on my way to getting unstable as well. "You and your damn father."

I called another objection. "Objection. Badgering the witness."

Caplan tried to appeal to my sensitivities then.

"If you love her, think about what she's going to feel if she wakes up and watches this testimony. Think about how betrayed she's going to feel."

We were reaching new lows. I felt like if I didn't play ball, he could very well go to the hospital and pull the plug on her tonight. But I couldn't look Lauren's almost killer in the face and do anything to help him. Even as he appealed to my sensitivities about her. I couldn't bring myself to do anything for this monster. I rose from my seat, straightening my tie, and pushed passed the man standing in my way. Nobody stopped me as I made my exit from the trial room. This trial was trashed, and everyone knew it.

Think about how betrayed she's going to feel.

I was already thinking about all of that.

When I showed up to court that morning, I knew exactly how to hit Caplan where he'd feel it.

His job.

I knew if I got on the stand and did the opposite of what he was expecting me to do, it wouldn't be long before he began to feel like his job was on the line. Joshua Caplan, I'd come to learn, cared about his position more than anything else—even his own daughter. The moment he felt it was threatened by a humiliating witness, he would lose his composure—as he did. This would ultimately be his downfall.

But it would ultimately be mine as well.

Because one day Lauren would wake up, and believing it was Silas who was the reason she was shot, and not her own father, she would see the aftermath of my testimony. She would see it as me defending the man who tried to kill her.

And I knew that would destroy her.

Chapter Two

KAIN

Joshua Caplan would make history after all.

His trial would be the trial used for decades to explain why prosecutors should not have personal connections to anyone in the cases they try. The legal blunder of the era. It must've been humiliating. News anchors across networks seemed to relish in the unprofessionalism of the spectacle he put on, playing his outbursts about Lauren over and over and over, making him look like a mad man.

"Let us remind the viewers that the case has nothing to do with the Florida prosecutor's daughter," a female news anchor informed, shaking her head a little before a muted version of Joshua Caplan screaming in court flashed across the screen.

"Jenna, I don't think we're talking about Kain Montgomery enough," the male anchor beside her added. "At just twenty-one years old, the pre-law Florida State University senior held his own against a seasoned law veteran, issuing accurate objections for his own questioning. A law career may have crashed and burned today, but one has certainly risen from the ashes. We're all very eager to see where the young man goes in life."

"Lest you all forget, the young man's father, Silas Montgomery, who won his trial today is still behind bars tonight, awaiting trial for an alleged shooting of Joshua Caplan's daughter sometime next year. Silas Montgomery remains the only suspect in the shooting, and in true Romeo and Juliette fashion, Joshua Caplan's daughter just so happened to be in a serious relationship with our young future lawyer. Kain Montgomery was the one who called the paramedics for her at the time of her shooting. Isn't that absolutely crazy?"

"The plot thickens!"

"You're absolutely right, Dave." Jenna smiled brightly at her partner as if they were reading off such a lighthearted story. "It's a pity that law school is a four-year commitment. If Silas Montgomery had his son defending his next case, that would've been a saga for the ages."

"You're getting ahead of yourself here, Jenna. Kain is a college senior this upcoming fall and according to some sources, he hasn't even taken the LSAT yet, much less applied to any schools."

"Well, I know one thing is for sure, Dave. After what happened this morning, Kain Montgomery is going to have the law schools sending *him* all the love calls, not the other way around. Viewers, we've put a poll up on our Twitter page. Where do you think Kain Montgomery should go to law schoo—"

I changed the channel, opting for a more local news cast. A reporter was standing just outside of Jackson Memorial Hospital, and my posture straightened up, bringing up the remote to raise the volume of the story being told.

"Yes, we're just now being told by staff within the hospital that after just about two weeks on life support, Lauren Caplan, nineteen-year-old daughter of disgraced Miami prosecutor Joshua Caplan, is breathing on her own. There's no word on whether or not she's risen from her drug-induced coma, but the IV bags that had been delivering her medications have been removed. It should only be an hour or so before she comes to."

The field report cut to a studio where a lone anchor sat behind a desk and continued with the story.

"These new installments come less than twenty-four hours after a distraught Joshua Caplan, likely overcome with grief, completely crashed his trial in a Miami-Dade courthouse early this morning against Silas Montgomery, Lauren's accused attempted murderer. A staple in the South Florida law community, many people who know Joshua Caplan best say that the pain over having his daughter on life support is likely what caused the courthouse blunder. We hope that with the reunion of father and daughter, justice can continue to be served efficiently in Miami-Da—Breaking News!"

A shot of the field report cut into the studio feed. My heartrate sped up.

"Lauren Caplan has reportedly opened her eyes! Lauren Caplan is finally awake."

* * *

Love will make you do dumb things.

It was two days after Lauren woke up when I decided to pay her a visit. I knew not to go there with expectations of actually seeing her. There wasn't a doubt in my mind that she believed that Silas was the person who shot her in cold blood, so it didn't surprise when I learned that I was the only person on her don't-let-through list. Now that she was awake, there really wasn't much my sister Monique could do to get me in that room without truly jeopardizing her job. I understood that Lauren needed to heal, so I didn't force myself in her space. Instead, I told myself that she couldn't shut me out forever.

I was wrong.

One week to the day that Lauren came back, after seven days of no contact, I woke up to a banging at my door. Silas was being held at the local prison, awaiting trial for Lauren's shooting, and I'd finally gotten around to giving Vance the house in Pembroke Pines. So I was at the big house alone that day. I don't know what I was expecting when I heard the loud knocking at the door from my room that morning. I'd be lying if I said a little part of me didn't have some hope that when I opened it, Lauren would be standing at the other side, ready to hear my side of the story.

Of course it wasn't her.

On the other side of the front door was a uniformed police officer, standing stocky and stiff at the door's threshold. Visibly, his neck craned ever so slightly in an effort to catch a glimpse at the inside of the house behind me—the infamous house of Silas Montgomery. I cleared my throat once, urging him to state his reason for being here. Was I under arrest? Was I needed for questioning?

None of that. Instead, from behind his back, the pale officer pulled a large manila envelope visible. I was being served papers.

"Kain Montgomery?" He confirmed my identity as a formality no doubt, 'cause there was no way he didn't already know. There wasn't a person in this city who didn't know who I was. When I nodded a confirmation, he extended the envelope into my hands, and I shut the door.

I'd walked with the envelope to the kitchen, both wanting to know immediately what was inside and wanting to know nothing at all. It wasn't until I'd brewed and poured myself a cup of coffee that I took a seat at the kitchen island, and began to peel back the adhered seal. There was only one sheet of paper inside, a legal document with Lauren's signature at the bottom.

A restraining order.

If nothing else, I wasn't surprised. Lauren believed Silas was the person behind her shooting, and I didn't have a doubt in my mind that the first thing Joshua Caplan updated her on upon her waking up was the scene

I'd made in court last week. To her, it must've felt like between her and my father, I had chosen my father.

Joshua Caplan didn't just shoot his daughter. He lied about it. He tried to use it to his advantage. And he didn't even seem remorseful. To tell Lauren the truth, was to make her aware of the extent her father was willing to go to come out on top—even if that meant killing her.

I knew that believing I'd betrayed her must've been hurting Lauren at that moment, and despite my ability to put an end to that belief, I made the decision to stand down. Why? Because telling her wouldn't take away the pain she was feeling at all. In fact, it might just make it worse.

Love makes you do dumb things.

How do I know? Because I looked at that sheet of paper for at least an hour, knowing deep down that if I could somehow tell Lauren the truth, that paper would become meaningless. But I wouldn't do that. Because how do you tell someone that their own father shot them in cold blood? Accidentally or not, Joshua Caplan shot his daughter, and if I found some way to tell Lauren everything I knew, I could rip up the restraining order quick, but I would be ripping her heart to shreds as well.

And under the influence of love—and stupidity, probably—the thought of breaking Lauren's heart in that way was more unbearable than the pain of my own heart breaking.

So I put the paper back in its envelope, finished my coffee, and decided to respect her wishes.

Fifteen Months Later

Chapter Three

Lauren

Men are trash.

Not some men.

All men.

Just trash.

I met Rashad Bordeaux at a country club mixer three months ago. He came from a good family—two doctors for parents and an older brother at a Top 5 law school. The Beauvais Country Club liked to throw these monthly mixers for young, single members to mingle. It was really just a poorly veiled scheme to encourage moneyed black youths to stick to their own kind—that is both rich and of color. Heaven forbid the good, privileged flock within *The Beauvais* walls marry into middle class black families—or worse, working class.

So for this, there was The Youth Mixer.

When I went to my first event ten months ago, I was a little worried I'd be a pariah. I'd only just got out of a very public relationship with the son of Miami's most infamous crime boss five months before. In my mind, this almost certainly made me "tainted goods". But alas, in these last few months I'd come to understand that men really only want three things. A pretty face, a nice ass, and a closed mouth—unless opened wide for the reception of dick, of course.

When it came to face, ass, and talkativeness, I checked off all the boxes. Ever since coming out of the hospital fifteen months ago, I just wasn't the talker I used to be. Despite the fact that I was absolutely "tainted goods," my unwillingness to speak unless necessary, paired with my face and body, turned out to make me one of the most popular participants at The Youth Mixer. Second only to my own twin sister.

Rashad Bordeaux was the ninth man at the club that I'd given the time of the day. I'd picked him, just like the last eight, because he had nothing in common with Him. Rashad was short—my height. Born from a family of Louisiana Creoles, he had skin so pale that he could pass for white. With his dark eyes and his sandy brown curls, there was nothing about him that resembled the man who haunted my memories.

That's how I liked it. All of them light. All of them short. And all of them self-absorbed.

Rashad was my ninth, but that did not make me a whore. Over the past year, I'd slept with very few of the men I'd entertained. If we were talking how many bodies I'd invited in since Kain, Rashad would be my third. They were to drown out the memories, done with the hope of forgetting Him. Three men got to explore my depths after Kain. I referred to them mentally as first, second, and third.

The second was because the first only made me remember Kain more. And the third—Rashad—he just so happened to be around when my loneliness got to be too overpowering.

The men I had been with didn't just differ from Kain in appearance alone. While I made efforts to be with men who had nothing in common with him, I'd gotten subpar sex as a side effect. These new hands differed in the ways that they touched me, fingers rabid and rough. They served themselves, primarily seeking their own pleasure, and then mine as an afterthought. They didn't pretend to love me. They never even tried to see me—not the real me, at least.

That's how I liked it.

If they could see me, then they would see how utterly unimpressed I was. Sometimes the sex was decent. Most of the time it couldn't even be that. However, when all the lights are off, a touch is a touch, a kiss is a kiss, and if they didn't speak, I wouldn't have to think about how their voices didn't sound like His.

Rashad, my third since Him.

He came after Nathan and Vergil, the fourth man to know the depths of my insides, and it only took him two weeks.

I wasn't particularly attracted to Rashad. But my parents liked him. They liked everyone I brought home ever since Him. But they really, *really* liked Rashad—more so than the other men that came before he came along, and definitely more than the first. Rashad made my parents laugh. He made them smile. This was something I no longer knew how to do, so I kept him around so that I wouldn't forget what their smiles looked like.

Rashad, who I called Shad, had a small apartment just outside of Downtown Miami, in a neighborhood that was being newly gentrified. He, of course, was the gentrifier in this equation, snagging a twentieth-floor condo overlooking the changing Overtown neighborhood skyline. The view was beautiful at night, so I found myself there often in the evenings.

We'd just returned from two Thanksgiving dinners—one at my parents' house and one at his grandmother's house. After a long night of awkward family encounters, we were in his apartment, trying to get in a lazy fuck before I called myself an Uber home. It was regular people stuff, I guess.

I kept my shirt on; something I only did when the man I was with insisted on keeping the lights on. Rashad's hands circled around my waist, grip a little too tight, a little too eager.

"Your parents were really feeling me at dinner tonight," he whispered against my neck. Great, because every woman wants to think about her parents just before she gets fucked. Rashad bit down on the delicate skin on my neck, and over his shoulder, I released a sigh.

To him it might've sounded like a satisfied breath, but it was really an expression of my own frustration. Unwanted conversation aside, Rashad, despite his best efforts, just didn't know how to touch me. All of his attempts to try new things only served to remind me of this fact.

"Baby—"

"I told you not to call me that," I interrupted softly, squirming under his hands slightly.

"Sweetheart," he corrected himself, allowing his hand to creep under the fabric of my shirt. "We've been doing it for at least two months now. Why are you still hiding from me?"

I hated that he was twenty-six and still referred to sex as *doing it*. In my moment of subtle irritation, I forgot to respond.

"Lauren?"

"You want me to take my shirt off?" I whispered hesitantly, pulling backward to look into his dark eyes. Looking into Rashad's eyes was like looking into an empty cave. There was nothing in them except, given the right lighting, my own reflection. With a silent nod, his hand crept further into the underside of my shirt. I drew in a sharp breath, but didn't allow my hands to come up to stop him.

The pale pink color of my top fell around us, and Rashad's eyes fell down to take in the exposure. He looked at my bare skin as though he was hungry, his tongue coming out to run between his pressed together lips. Saying nothing, he just took it all in, his face lowering to make sure he didn't miss an inch of me.

When he saw it, I knew.

Confused, his eyebrows came together questioningly before his features relaxed. I could almost see him remembering what everybody in the city knew.

Last year, I was shot. It didn't leave me dead, but it left me with a long, raised scar running along my ribcage in one clean line. The healed cut was nearly black in color, desperate to be seen and always succeeding. For a split second, Rashad's lip curled in subtle repulsion and as discretely as he could muster, his hand at my waist lowered as if he was trying not to touch it. The blemish was too ugly to touch.

My boyfriend looked at me like I was gross, and so I felt gross.

"It's not that bad," he assured, though I couldn't be sure if he was trying to convince me or himself. My arms came up to cover my exposed skin, and twice I swallowed to keep the cry rumbling in my chest from surfacing. "Lauren, it's really not that ba—"

"I don't want to do this anymore," I whispered, turning away from his staring to reach for my shirt. As my fingers wrapped around the fabric, I felt the point of his chin rest into the crook of my neck, his arms coming around me from behind, resting just over my breasts.

"Sweetheart, it's not the end of the world," he whispered into the silence of the room, his voice tiredly pleading. "You're beautiful," he assured. "It's not like that thing is on your face, right?"

That thing.

I felt like I might throw up.

"I'm going home," I announced with a shaky voice. My shoulders squirmed as I tried to wiggle out of his grip. Rashad's arms around me only tightened. "Shad, let me go."

"Don't be like this," he kept his voice quiet, a whiny plea coloring his tone. "You got me all worked up, gorgeous. Just lie down on your stomach. I'll be quick, I promise."

He leaned forward with me in his arms, going lower and lower until I was left pinned under the weight of his body. My arms came up behind me in the hopes that I would get the point across if I smacked him around a few times. Pressing his body into my back, Rashad grabbed at my wrists, pinning them above my head with one firm hand. From behind me, I felt his other hand squeeze in between us, guiding his erection through the confusion of my kicking and squirming.

"I said no!"

He said nothing in response to my refusal, and he made no sudden movements to get off, snaking his erection between my thighs. His breath hit the back of my neck, hot and quick with anticipation. If he could see the tears forming in my eyes, he wasn't deterred by them.

"Rashad, *stop*. I don't—"

He pushed in, his erection roughly forcing into the dry skin of my unwilling body. I didn't scream. Instead I sunk my head into the pillow in front of me, turning my head towards the window at the far side of the room. Drowning out the sounds of Rashad's animalistic grunts, I focused on the view of Downtown Miami. It was dark outside, the city lit by dozens of lights that twinkled with the reminder that in that moment, life was going on all around me.

Each light was a person, a family, a group of friends. Maybe they were gathered around a dinner table and taking turns revealing what they were thankful for. What was I thankful for? A tear rolled down to the tip of my nose, my soul crumbling over the robbery taking place within me. My body wasn't mine in that moment, snatched from me in a painful violation that seemed to go on for hours.

All the while, I laid there silent, on my stomach, staring out the window of Rashad Bordeaux's apartment, taking in that beautiful Overtown skyline.

Chapter Four

KAIN

Silas had lost weight.

At least a good forty pounds, I decided from my end of the visitation table. I could see why, though, as Thanksgiving dinner for that evening consisted of four bags of potato chips he'd asked me to buy for him from the vending machine. In the fifteen months he'd been here awaiting trial for Lauren's shooting, today was the first time I'd visited him.

The visiting room was empty except for us, and the clock on the wall told me we were way past the visiting time window. Silas had to have pulled some strings to get this late night meeting. I pulled out an iron foldable chair.

"I didn't have that girl shot, you know," was the first thing he said to me when I sat down. Without a word, I nodded. I already knew this much. "So why you ain't been comin' to see me?" he asked, unable to sound anything but hurt.

"I've been busy with law school interviews," I replied, which wasn't a lie, but not entirely a good excuse. "And runnin' all these clubs and shit. It's been a lot."

That was a better excuse.

"From what I've heard, you done dropped all the girls." My father shook his head and split open a yellow bag of chips in front of him. He'd heard correctly. The drugs, I could keep up with, but I couldn't make time to give attention to the network of pimps and prostitutes my father profited from. Nor did I want to. "You leavin' a lot of money on the table, Kain."

"Yeah." I nodded, leaning back in my seat and welcoming whatever harsh string of words he had ready for me. The tongue lashing never came. Surprisingly, Silas' shoulders relaxed. He changed the subject.

"Vance told me you've been workin' on startin' up a record label with Marlon." It was Thanksgiving and my shrinking father really just wanted to sit and make small talk with me. I didn't feel guilty for not having visited sooner, but something in me did sink. Perhaps it was because I had to remind myself that even though Silas probably did deserve to be in here, he was innocent of the crime he was accused of. "How's Marlon been? You heard from his mama?"

I chuckled at his last question, reaching for a bag of chips in front of me.

"Give it up, Dad. Marie don't want your old ass no more. And Marlon's a'ight. He finally got that PhD in communications, so it's *Doctor* Marlon Xavier now."

"Yeah, he told me last time he came by." Marlon hadn't told me he'd visited my father in prison, but I didn't exactly ask. I could see why he would do it. Even though Marlon had harsh opinions about Silas, my father was as close to a father as he ever had growing up. "So a record label?"

"It just sort of happened." I shrugged. "Marlon had the plans mapped out and he just needed the funding behind it. So came *Montgomery Records* and he was named CEO. I thought it was about time. There's money in music."

"Clean money," Silas heard the hidden meaning behind my words. "Is that why you closed all the whore houses? Are the drugs next? You tryna get out the game?"

"I don't know, Dad. I'm just tired all the time, and with law school coming up next—"

"Boy, *fuck* law school!" He slammed the bag in his hand down violently. This was the answer he was trying to get out of me, and now that he'd gotten it, he was furious. "I worked hard buildin' up this city, and you not gon' fuck it up because you wanna run around and play *Law and Order* at Yale, or wherever."

"Vance told you about that, too, huh?" Why should I be surprised that Vance told him about Yale? That might've been something to brag about for him, but to Silas, it was a waste of time.

"When I get outta here, I'm not tryna play around with some music shit. It's money in music, but it ain't never gon' be nothin' compared to pushin' product and pussy, you hear me? You keep my money in check till I get back."

"I don't think you're gettin' out of here," I hit him with the truth. "Lauren—" It still burned my tongue to say her name "—is fully cooperating in the case against you. It's her word against yours, and she has story after story that shows you wanted her dead."

"But that's *your* bitch, right?" I inwardly cringed. "Well you find her, and tell her it was her fuckin' Pops who blew that hole through her. You can fix this mess you made if you want to, Kain."

If I want to...

"She'd never believe that," I explained, leaning over the table's surface. "*Especially* coming from me, after what I did to her father's career last year. Dad, if you want to beat this, we gotta find some way to make him confess, and I bet he'd rather die than let his family see him that way."

Silas shook his head, irritated with my response.

"You not tryin' hard enough," he told me. In truth, I wasn't trying at all. Silas being in prison, though I'd never say it out loud, hadn't exactly depressed me as much as it depressed everyone else in my family. My days were peaceful. My nights were predictable. There wasn't an aging father over my shoulder who I felt bound to out of respect.

Silas was in prison.

But I was finally free.

"I'll try to visit more often, Dad."

And I let that be the last thing I said to him.

* * *

Eden sings like an angel.

It was a Friday evening at a one-room jazz club in the heart of the city—family-owned of course. Eden Xavier was giving a debut live performance of all the songs on her upcoming album for a room of music journalists, bloggers, and influencers. She was very much in her element.

When Eden gets lost in a song, she closes her eyes and tosses her head back slightly. Her tongue creeps out to glaze her lips just before every high note. And like always, the room shakes into a somehow audible silence. People watch her, enamored by the harmonies she spins with ease, but when her head bowed to the closing of the song, her opened eyes scanned the crowd and ultimately stopped on me. She stared me down, an eyebrow climbing over the fact that I was the only one in the room not clapping.

I broke eye contact, checking my phone for any new messages, and to remind myself that I could have any woman in this city that I wanted.

Except for two.

Marlon's little sister was definitely off-limits.

And the other? Well, I couldn't get within one-hundred yards of her. I had the restraining order to prove it.

The lit screen in my hand glowed with three unread text messages, each of them asking if I wanted them to stop by tonight. I thought about it, trying to decide if I wanted the company. It was a little after midnight, and from the energy of the crowd, I just knew Eden's album release party was going to be a long one if she wanted it to be.

Marlon's sister was the first artist signed to the label we'd started a few months before. After getting his PhD in communications with prime focus in emerging media and entertainment marketing, Marlon was convinced he had just the right combination of tools and skill to take the music industry by storm. From the look of the media coverage he'd managed to secure for Eden's private show, I believed it. He was the brains; I was the bank. Thus, *Montgomery Records* was born.

"You texting one of your hos?"

I looked up from my phone at the sound of Eden's question, the teasing quality in her tone not all the way genuine. She actually was curious; maybe a little jealous, too.

Eden and I were same age, but it was easy to forget from the way her brown eyes always seemed to shine with mischief. Like her older brother, I'd spent my childhood with her, all the time seeing her like an honorary younger sister—that is, until she got older and started flirting with me.

While I didn't discourage the attention, I can't say that I welcomed it either. Eden was a gray area woman in my life. I'd seen way too much of her growing up—from taking loose teeth out from under her pillow to teaching her how to drive. Even though she wasn't, she was practically my sister.

Then she went away to Berklee to study music, staying gone for four years. After graduating, she came back to Miami two inches taller and a couple inches thicker, no longer the little girl I grew up with. It was only then that I couldn't help but remember that Eden wasn't my sister at all.

But she was Marlon's little sister for sure.

Honestly, if I had well-meaning intentions, it wouldn't have been a problem to welcome Eden's flirting. However, lately, I wasn't looking for anything meaningful. Just trying to have fun, I wasn't really trying to build anything with anyone.

The women behind the texts in my phone knew this, and although I could feel them attempting to change my mind, to inspire love out of me, I was quick to remind them to stop trying. I could be that way with them because they knew what they were signing up for, but I wouldn't do it to Eden.

"I don't have hos, Eden." She rolled her eyes at the obvious lie, setting her mic down on the table in front of me and pulling out the second seat. "Don't you have interviews to give?"

"They can wait."

I chuckled. "Spoken like a true star."

"You weren't impressed with my performance, huh?" she asked, grabbing a bit of her straight hair, twisting the brown and green strand around her finger. Objectively speaking, Eden was beautiful. Her mid-toned brown skin looked like she got the right amount of sunlight year-round, even though we were late into November. She had a face that kind of reminded me of a 90s-era Jada Pinkett Smith, and when she smiled her big brown eyes lit up in a way that was vaguely familiar.

"The performance was fine," I assured.

"I didn't see you clapping." I set my phone down and clapped for her quietly, which made her frown. "You heard my voice crack on that second note, didn't you?"

"I didn't." I did hear it, but it was her first ever live performance. For her to have been perfect would have been unrealistic. "You keep these interviewers waitin' any longer, and you're gonna wake up to bad reviews on your album."

"Are you taking me home after this?" she asked, eyebrows raised and eager. I sighed, tossing a glance at Eden's manager far behind her, and pulled out my phone to let her know I was taking Eden home. Eden's smile steadily grew as I typed out the message, and she was practically beaming when I hit send. "Great! I'll make this quick and meet you at your car."

"You're always so grumpy, you know that?" Eden informed from the passenger's seat of my car. She had the seat kicked back and her bare feet up on the dashboard. "You never used to be like this."

"Like what?"

Eden shrugged, tapping a beat on her raised knees before simply saying, "Sad."

I didn't reply to her observation, rounding a corner in silence. It wasn't until I stopped at a red light when she said something else.

"What's your twenties without a broken heart one or two times?" Her hand was on my shoulder—not in a suggestive manner, but so that I'd look away from the road and at her. "You don't heal by fucking randoms and never letting people in again."

"Eden," there was warning in my tone, "I'm not doing this with you. You're out your lane. Get back in it."

These kinds of conversations were what I paid my therapist for. Eden huffed from her side of the car, her hand still on my shoulder, but not saying anything. Although I would've preferred not to be touched, I was at least grateful for the silence. From my periphery, I could see Eden's head turned toward the side of my face the entire time, watching me carefully. Pretty as she was, there weren't many things about her that reminded me of *Her*.

Over the past fifteen months, I'd developed something I never used to have before.

A type.

Eden's shoulder length, pin straight brown hair with the forest green ends, was a far cry from the natural heads of big black curls I'd grown to prefer. Eden was just about two shades too light, three inches too short, and ten pounds too thin. She didn't have dimples when she smiled. When she got uncomfortable, she'd get quieter instead of talking more. Although her eyes were big and the right shade of brown, they just weren't the same.

Not even close.

"Could you stop staring at me?" I broke the silence, not taking my eyes off the road. Eden swiped her hand off my shoulder and sunk into her seat. We were about five minutes out from her Miami Beach apartment, and from the clock on my dashboard, I knew I was going to be late getting back home.

"Do you chase me away because of Marlon?" Eden asked suddenly, her voice a cross between wounded and curious. "Because you're worried that if you give your best friend's little sister the time of day, he'll turn on you?"

I sighed. "It's not like that."

"Then tell me what it's like."

"We don't want the same things, Eden." I gave it to her straight. "You out here lookin' for a man who will make you the center of his universe, am I right?"

She cleared her throat, awkwardly replying, "That would be nice."

"Well, I'm not in the market for a center to my universe. I'm just lookin' for distractions right now."

"What are they distracting you from?"

I shrugged, pulling in to a roadside drop-off loop off a tall apartment building, telling Eden what I told my therapist. "The past." I nodded towards the door. "You're home."

She didn't immediately get out of the car. "Kain, I'm so hungry."

"Thanksgiving was yesterday," I reminded. "You don't have leftovers?"

Eden made a face.

"Don't be rude," she snapped. "I was in the studio all day yesterday recording background vocals for today. And I haven't eaten in like forty-eight hours because I was trying to look good in this dress tonight. I'm *literally* starving."

"It's after midnight."

"I know a place by the beach that is still open. Just drive and I'll tell you when to turn."

My eyes darted to the clock on my dashboard. It was fifteen minutes to one o'clock in the morning. I had someone waiting for me outside my apartment, and even though I was sure she'd still be there when I got home, the unexpected detour for the night had my patience wearing thin.

"You trying to get home to one of your hos?"

"As a matter of fact, I am."

Wrinkling her nose, Eden crossed her arms and sunk further into her seat. She wasn't budging. Sighing in frustration, I gave in and pulled the car out of park. We'd get her something to-go and call it a night.

"Booty calls at one o'clock in the morning." She chuckled at the observation. "You wanna call her and tell her you're about to be late?"

"She'll wait."

"*Wow.*" Eden's loud outburst bounced off the interior of my car, having the car vibrating in her outrage as she repeated the word. "Wow. Wooooooow. You are a *literal* fuckboy, you know that?"

I dodged the statement, handing Eden my phone. "Put the restaurant into the GPS."

"Hey *Siri*," Eden called into my phone. "Find the quickest route to Catfish Carol's."

I flinched, an involuntary reaction, before I took my phone back and simply stated, "I know where it is."

"Since when do you like seafood?"

I shrugged, not wanting to get too deep into it. Eden didn't need to know the answer to *every* damn thing. Eden didn't need to know that I knew where the restaurant was because Catfish Carol's was Lauren's number one choice as well.

The familiar roads to what was once Lauren's favorite place to grab a bite, were still fresh in my memory, each turn sending me into flashbacks of last summer. Images of Lauren in the passenger's seat of my car, saying something or another about whatever was on her mind that day. If I focused hard enough, I could make out the sound of her voice as if it was her beside me now.

What was it that Lauren used to say? She always had so much to say, but now I couldn't remember any of it. How could her words be scattered to the wind, but her voice in my mind still clear as day? It was a strange kind of memory, vivid yet somehow incomplete.

I wondered if the longing that burned in my chest was displayed on my face. I hated that even after all this time, it left me feeling hollow to even allow my mind to wander to her. I could feel Eden's eyes on me as I weaved through the tangled Miami streets. If she could tell that I was having my own mental journey as we took this literal one, she didn't make the observation known.

The short detour to the beachside eatery was a quiet one, the images outside my window making me feel heavy with nostalgia. There were so many memories in this part of town. When I parked outside of the neon-colored storefront, my eyes wandered to the end of a curb. As if it were real, ghosts of me and Lauren walked along the familiar sidewalk, headed for the ocean.

This was where Lauren and I had our first date.

More than a year and a half ago, we walked this path, stopped on a bed of beach sand... And I... It was all downhill for me from there. I could remember her back against my chest as we watched the waves die inches away from where we sat. There was the gradual slowing of her breaths when she relaxed, as she began to feel comfortable in the space between my arms. I was always so aware of Lauren's breathing, the way she always seemed to unconsciously match each of her inhales with mine.

Unfortunately, I could also remember her lips. The first time was memorable, the way they cautiously touched mine with a curious shyness that dispersed within seconds. I remembered feeling like there was no way I'd just met this girl less than a week before. I kissed Lauren with the kind of passion that used to take me months of interaction to develop for someone. It came naturally for her. Later it would occur to me that perhaps my mind didn't know I would love her someday.

But my soul knew.

I killed the engine of my car, tossing a pressing look Eden's way.

"What?" she questioned. "You're not getting out of the car with me?"

I started to lose the little patience I had left. "Eden..."

"It's best when it's fresh. If I order takeout, I am going to eat it in your car. And if I'm not mistaken, you hate the smell of fish." She shrugged, giving me an ultimatum. "You want the smell in your car, or do you want to suffer through it for, like, twenty minutes while I eat?"

It would've been nothing to tell the woman in front of me that I'd call her an Uber back to her place and get on with the rest of my night. However, it was late, and this was *Eden*, not some random woman I picked up through some chance encounter. Even though she was seriously testing my limits, I couldn't just leave her here. Some part of me, in a vaguely brotherly way, loved this annoying ass brat. I wouldn't just leave her here.

So, with that, I unbuckled my seatbelt, scowling at the sound of Eden clapping her hands with excitement.

"Our first date," she giggled.

Chapter Five

Lauren

"Do you have a driver's license, ma'am?"

The tech behind the pharmacy counter popped her gum along with her question, the two-inch acrylics on her nails digging into and denting the cardboard packaging of the pill I was trying to buy. I held up a finger for her to wait as I opened up my purse in search of some identification. In the state of Florida, you had to be at least seventeen years old to legally buy *Plan B* emergency contraceptive.

Today, however, I was far from home. I didn't want to be recognized by anyone in the vicinity, so I'd taken an hour long drive cross-county and found myself at the counter of a sleepy town's *Walgreens* pharmacy. The store was already decorated in anticipation of the Christmas holiday.

It was the second time in my life that I was buying the morning after pill. However, today would be the first time I actually took it.

Rashad and I had unprotected sex.

That, at least, was what I kept telling myself. Images of me pinned under him, powerless to stop the violation that took place two days before, seemed to take a backseat in the evaluation of what had actually happened. I refused to call it what it was. Instead, I simply kept telling myself that Rashad and I had unprotected sex, highlighting the fact that the main mistake of that evening was not in that we had one-sided sex, but that he wasn't wearing a condom. To focus on anything else would have seriously fucked with my mental health.

So, I just...didn't.

Once upon a time, I narrowly escaped a very similar incident. However, if I was being real, how similar would the experiences have been? I didn't know the first man who tried to forcibly have me. I knew Rashad, however. In fact, Rashad was my boyfriend. I would've said I knew him well. Somehow, I was unsure if this made what he did to me better or worse.

He didn't do anything to you.

My inner thoughts berated me for forgetting to remember this.

It wasn't rape.

It was unprotected sex.

The reminders came with repetition, sounding off in my head as if to convince me of something rather than to remind. That night, after he was done, Rashad rolled off of me with a grunt, forcing out a breath and something that sounded like a mumbled apology. I pretended not to hear it. To acknowledge his apology would have made me acknowledge that he had done something he needed to be sorry for.

And like I said, Rashad did not rape me.

We had unprotected sex.

That is all.

Nothing more. Nothing less. Nothing to apologize for. The only thing that needed to be done was buy this stupid, stupid pill. That would fix everything and then I could just forget all of this.

And I *would* forget it.

Easily.

Because this certainly wasn't the worst thing to ever happen to me. A little over a year ago, I gave my virginity over to a total monster. He allowed me to think he loved me. Hell, he even told me he loved me once. He grew to know the depths of my body, and he really had me fooled, taking more than just my virginity in the process.

Kain had my heart. My whole heart.

I was so in love.

And then his father had me shot in cold blood.

It was a warm July morning outside a club where we'd been celebrating his birthday. I'd given my body to him that night as well, one last time among the dozens of times I'd shared myself with him that summer.

I lost so much that morning. That night I lost literal parts of my body, I lost my peace of mind, and hear my mother tell it, I nearly lost my own life. When I woke up, I learned I'd lost the life growing within me, a life that was half his. And lastly, I lost him.

But perhaps, given the fact that he'd been the one to hold my dying body in his hands, and then still take the stand and defend the man who'd done it to me... Perhaps I never actually had Kain in the first place.

Say you love me, and then go on to protect the man who tried to kill me.

Even now, I still couldn't understand the lack of humanity it took to be so...cold.

I gave my virginity to that.

So, all things considered, even though what went down with Rashad created a gnawing feeling in the pit of my chest, it certainly wasn't the worst thing that ever happened to me. Something might've been taken from me a couple nights ago, but it would never measure up to what was taken from me that summer.

After everything I'd been through, as both a blessing and a curse, it would take so much more to break me down. I certainly wasn't the girl Kain found pinned to his bed nearly two years ago. The woman I'd become had a hard exterior and the lowest of expectations when it came to men.

My only concern right now was making sure I didn't get tied down by a baby I didn't want, with a man I *certainly* didn't want.

I pulled out my debit card to pay for the pill, my eyes wandering to a rack of gossip magazines for sale at the register. As the Plan B was being bagged for me, I stopped at a cover that made my heart sink. As if to torture myself, I found my hands reaching for the booklet, adding its price to my total.

"I'll take the magazine, too."

Eden Xavier was being called this generation's Lauryn Hill.

She wrote her own songs. She played her own instruments. She was an artist to the bone, fresh out of the Berklee College of Music up north. There was no doubting that Eden Xavier was talented.

I liked her music, the last two singles she released ahead of her debut album, *EX*, were in my music library and I knew all the words. If anyone had asked me any time before today, I might've called myself a fan. Though, I'd never really cared much to do any research on her. For all I cared to pay attention to, she was just another face in the ever-evolving music industry. I didn't even know who she was signed to. When it came to Eden Xavier, I'd never been given much of a reason to look beyond her music.

Until now.

The magazine on my lap displayed a gorgeous photo of her. Eden had the most flawlessly sun-kissed brown skin, matching well with her green highlighted, honey brown hair that stopped just above her shoulders. Some girls are just objectively pretty by any standards. Eden was one of those girls, as most people in the entertainment industry needed to be. Split down the middle of the magazine cover, another face was photographed.

His.

The headline and subtitle written above the two side-by-side photos, on the cover of *Fame Weekly*, read: *Friends in High Places? How Eden Xavier's Romance with Kain Montgomery Might be the Secret to Her Success.*

This wouldn't be the first time I'd found myself alone in my car, reading some gossip piece on Him. More times than I cared to admit, I found myself checking blogs and magazines like *Fame Weekly* for tidbits into a life I was no longer a part of. There had been stories about Kain being seen with a woman here, a woman there, but this story felt different.

Different because Eden and I had nothing in common.

At least, not physically.

The women Kain had been linked to before her... They looked like me. At least—they looked like the me he used to know. All of them were dark brown, big haired, with slim thick figures. I didn't look so much like that anymore.

I'd lost so much weight when I was in the hospital, and after waking up, the depression that followed made gaining it back damn near impossible. My desire to be outside was nonexistent—so naturally I grew paler than I used to be. My wild mane of curls was kept lowkey these days, pulled back or up into conservative buns that kept my hair out of my way.

Kain was pursuing clones of the girl I used to be, not realizing that wasn't even me anymore. If he'd developed a type, I no longer fit that mold.

However, neither did Eden.

And perhaps that was why I felt a heaviness in my chest. His connection with her marked a meaningful switch in his preferences, a clear sign that he had likely moved on. I couldn't be sure why I was so pressed. Even if he hadn't moved on, it wasn't like I wanted him anyway. He defended the man who tried to kill me, for God's sake.

And yet...

I cracked open the booklet, swiftly turning to the pages that held the cover article. The article was clearly written by someone heavily in favor of the pairing. The author threw around terms like *power couple*, *love*, and *soulmate*, completely ignoring the obvious story the photos of them told.

Kain didn't look interested.

They didn't look good together.

I didn't feel that way due to some childish kind of jealousy, either. In the candid shots of them tucked away in the corner of some vaguely familiar diner, Kain looked bored, looking down at a menu, as her undivided attention rested solely on him. If pictures could speak, they would say he wasn't even a little bit into her. Still, I finished reading the short article, learning a few things I didn't know before.

Eden Xavier was evidently the younger sister of Kain's business partner, Dr. Marlon Xavier. I squinted, recognizing the name immediately.

Marlon? As in the Marlon that Kain introduced me to over a year ago? His friend, Marlon?

I vaguely recalled Kain once telling me that Marlon and his siblings had lived with him when he was growing up. Was Eden some childhood first love that he'd eventually gravitated back to? Was she the girl I always thought he needed—worldly and unfazed by the horrors of his inner circle because she'd grown up around them, too?

Was she *The One*? Did he lie awake at night, watching her sleep and wondering how he could ever have given any other woman his time? Were the love songs on the *EX* album about him?

Why did I even care?

Tossing the magazine in the passenger's seat beside me, I leaned forward for my purse and pulled out a bottle of water. The one-dose package in my hand brought back distant memories of a summer that felt decades ago. This time, I didn't bother reading the side effects of the emergency pill. Instead, I uncapped my water and in one fell swoop, I got rid of any possibility of giving birth to Rashad's mistake.

Chapter Six

Lauren

Lux made sure I saw her checking the time on her watch when I finally arrived for coffee.

"You look a mess," she informed as I took my seat directly across from her in a quiet Brickell Village Starbucks. Lux, if nothing else, was always honest. And she could be especially harsh about it when her patience wore thin. She reached across to grab her venti raspberry iced tea, taking a long sip before she asked, "Did you already take the pill?"

Wordlessly, I nodded, dipping the teabag in my mug casually.

Although Luxana was my best friend, lately, there were things about myself that I kept hidden from her. She had no idea that I had already been pregnant once before. She didn't know about my miscarriage. And while she *did* know that I had taken Plan B this morning, she didn't know what Rashad had done.

"If you and Shad had a baby, it would be so cute, though." It didn't escape my notice that although she'd been the one to encourage me to '*do what I had to do*', Luxana sounded almost disappointed now. I thought about the reality of getting pregnant by a man who pinned me under the weight of his body and took me by force. I thought about whether or not I would ever be able to separate the encounter from the identity of said child.

No.

Probably not.

Instead, I cracked a smile and replied, "Maybe when I'm ready."

"Yeah," she agreed, leaning into the whitewashed wood table between us. "With your father running for governor and all, I bet it would've been a nasty scandal."

I frowned, reminded that even though my father had long left his high profile job as Miami-Dade County's state attorney, the time he'd taken off had only been spent preparing to take on an even more public position.

Governor of the great state of Florida.

Last year, after Kain Montgomery had humiliated my father in a court scene that would go on to ruin his career, Dad found himself known by just about everyone in the country. His courtroom antics had gone viral. A picture of his shouting face had even been a popular meme on Black Twitter for at least three months. His days as a lawyer were thrown to the dogs in a blink of an eye, and all he had to show for nearly twenty-five years of hard work was a legacy of infamy and humiliation.

Naturally, with no law career prospects and nationwide fame, my father decided to go into the only field where all publicity would be seen as good publicity.

Politics.

Credibility for sure played a part in American politics. However, the political golden goose would always be in one thing—name recognition. After the courtroom debacle with Kain last year, my father had more name recognition than the other gubernatorial candidates combined.

When people don't know who to vote for, they always pick the name they recognize.

This fact was plainly displayed in the way my father lead in the polls by double digits since announcing his run for governor five months ago.

He ran with issues that bordered on progressive and conservative, attracting the interest of both sides of the political spectrum. Dad promised to be tough on crime, soft on students, and raise teacher wages. Name recognition surely pulled people in, but his stances were what kept them in his corner.

My father's campaign was looking very good. He was realistically on track to becoming the first African-American governor of Florida, so naturally, he did everything he could to keep me out of the limelight.

To anyone who hadn't done their research, it would almost seem like my father only had one daughter. Rarely was I ever mentioned by name in his press releases. Common sense told me that this was because one would only have to Google me in order to find dozens of juicy blog posts from yesteryear's past, highlighting my relationship with the son of Miami's notorious crime boss.

Dad hoped to allow people to forget that I was ever wrapped up in the world of the Montgomery crime family. So, for this, he pushed Morgan to the forefront of his campaign—his beautiful, aspiring lawyer daughter, who pledged the right sorority, wore the right hairstyles, and hadn't dated anyone named Kain Montgomery. My only job was to be invisible, to not draw negative attention to the family...again.

So my parents encouraged me to date my boyfriend from "the right family", go to class and get good grades, and conveniently be "sick" every time Dad had a campaign event. Getting pregnant by said boyfriend, no matter how "right" his family was, certainly was not on the short list of things my parents wanted me to do.

I sipped at my tea quietly, choosing to say nothing even as my best friend raised her eyebrows with expectation. I only stared back, silent within the orchestra of coffeeshop sounds that surrounded us. As if to keep me on my toes, the universe decided to harass me then.

"He lied so beautifully, and I fell, fell stupidly..."

I scoffed at the opening lyrics of the song I used to love. Eden Xavier's album was officially out, and was being played to death all over the world. According to Billboard, *EX* was a love letter to the men of Eden's past— exes, if you will. The first single off the album had been released for months, titled, *He Lies*. Before today, I'd bumped the single at least once a car ride, singing along at the top of my lungs to a man who couldn't hear the words.

That song was so relatable.

But now all I could do was roll my eyes to the sound of Eden's uniquely soulful voice.

"What?" Luxana was taken aback by my reaction. "I thought you loved this song."

"Did you?" I sipped at my tea, my aura defensive. Even though nothing had been done to me, I suddenly found myself low on patience.

"Is this because Kain took her to Catfish Carol's?"

The question hit me like a rough punch to the stomach. "Took her *where*?"

Luxana nodded, rolling her eyes at my response. "I knew it. You saw the magazine article about Kain and Eden Xavier."

I repeated my question. "He took her where?"

"To the same restaurant you two had your first date at. You didn't notice from the pictures?" The restaurant in the photo had looked vaguely familiar, but I likely blocked the possibility of him taking her there out of my mind. *Of all the places...*

Lux's eyes widened at the realization that the truth was hitting me for the first time in that moment, her eyebrows dipping apologetically. Even though she didn't say so, I was sure she was sorry to be the bearer of bad news.

I could only shake my head with a shrug, trying to seem unfazed.

Over the past year and a half, I'd regularly been seeing a therapist. Recently, I was sure Dr. Eloise was the only person in the world that knew I lied awake at night and thought about him, thought about what I missed while we were apart, thought about what I did wrong.

Lux wouldn't see my eyes water over this. The past year had taught me that my emotions made the people around me uncomfortable. It was in everyone's best interest if I simply took life's emotional blows in stride. And, for the most part, that's what I did. I couldn't remember the last time I'd cried in front of my friends or family.

My therapist, however...

She'd better get the tissues ready.

* * *

Marlon met my straight face with skepticism.

Rarely did gossip magazines ever cause a blip in my day-to-day routine, but today things were a little different. Marlon stood before me not as a friend, not as a business partner, but as a concerned older brother.

"I don't care what it is you're going through these last few months with your *thot* rotation, but *my sister—*"

I stopped Marlon right there. "Save your energy."

Marlon slammed a copy of *Fame Weekly* onto his desk, displaying a candid shot of Eden and I at Catfish Carol's, the night of her album listening party. The article title was alluding to the possibility that Eden was sleeping with higher ups in exchange for music industry favor—higher ups, meaning me, in this equation.

I took a seat in the chair situated at the front of his workspace, replying, "How about you release a statement that says I grew up with Eden and she's practically my sister?"

Which was the truth.

Marlon leaned backwards against his desk. "I plan on it."

"Okay, so?"

"I need to hear it from you—man to man. Is Eden your latest stop in *the Let's Forget About Lauren* Tour?"

I scoffed, coughing back a laugh along with a simultaneous cringe. "Shut *the fuck* up."

This music exec shit was starting to make Marlon's analogies kind of insufferable. I narrowed my eyes at my friend, unsure if I was supposed to be taking this seriously. His expression didn't fall.

"It's *Eden*..." I stressed, my delivery almost disgusted, as if the mere thought of touching her made my skin crawl. *Shit*... it kinda did. Marlon could only look at me, an air of mistrust clouding over in his eyes. "Are you serious right now?"

"Just answer the question."

"I'm not fuckin' your kid sister."

"Are you trying to?"

Self-respect wouldn't even let me entertain the question. "Why don't you ask Eden why we were at that restaurant at one o'clock in the morning?"

"Bruh, I'm asking you."

"I would've never taken her there." *Especially there.*

Marlon's high-rise office in the heart of Miami's Arts & Entertainment District grew silent. When my countenance did not falter, the older brother bravado simmered down. Marlon was practically family, but I refused to let him even try to intimidate me. It wasn't in my nature to concede to anyone—not even my friends. As far as I could remember, there had only ever been one person who could make me stand down.

"Eden was hungry. I took her to a seafood place, and she ate there because I wasn't tryna have my car smell like the ocean." Marlon's shoulders relaxed and I assumed that meant this discussion was over.

"So there's no attraction at all?" he pressed, like a *TMZ* cameraman. I could only squint at this, irritation beginning to rise up from within. I was really not trying to have an hour-long conversation about the likelihood of me fucking Eden, *of all people.* "Eden's a pretty girl."

"Which ain't exactly rare," I countered. If he thought he was making a point, I'd be sure to let him know he had none. I could get pretty any day of the week. "I don't want your sister, bruh."

Marlon nodded at this, offering up a terse, "Good."

Even though it was a short response, I could see him gearing up to add on to that. From the way he shifted uncomfortably where he stood, I could tell he was about to come at me with some bullshit.

"What if the label doesn't release a statement?"

Right. Just as I suspected. Some bullshit.

I caught on quickly.

"Don't involve me on some media marketing project theory. You wanted the label—I invested. We not about to go back and forth on some '*All publicity is good publicity*' shit. Release the statement, or I will."

Marlon stood up straight, going into negotiating mode. I rose to my feet as well because I was not about to be pulled into this argument *literally* sitting down.

"Look, Eden's album shot up three spots on the charts. And the single that she released months ago is back in the Top 20. It's being played all over the city, too. This is organic growth with staying power. People who have never paid attention to her before are—"

"I don't give a *fuck*."

"Okay, we'll release a statement." *Well, that concession was quick.* "But let it be vague."

Skeptical, a single eyebrow rose. "How vague?"

"We keep everything as is, but we cut out the part about how you see her as your sister." Marlon could sense me about to decline, and so he continued. "Eden is the only artist on the label with mass market appeal right now. When her career takes off, then we can really begin leveraging her influence for other artists. Right now, it's a money drain and just because you don't care about blowing millions of dollars on a gamble, doesn't mean I don't. Even if it is your money—I did not get my PhD in this shit to not see results."

Marlon eyed me cautiously, bracing himself for an adamant refusal. I was just short of dismissing the idea once and for all, when I remembered my visit with Silas a few days prior.

For months, the new record label had been exactly as Marlon described it, a money drain. The money lost wasn't breaking anyone's bank, but the biggest takeaway from all of that wasn't in the fact that the label was expensive. The fact of the matter was that hopes and dreams wouldn't justify the losses forever. I could funnel as much money as I wanted into this project, but until the label started to keep itself afloat, I really had nothing to show for it. Everyday that we remained in the red, I lost my excuse to distance myself from the high risk businesses my family was known for.

I pushed out a sigh, something that Marlon immediately took for a yes, a triumphant smile spreading across his face in response to my scowl.

* * *

"So you're *not* dating the pop star," Dr. Eloise gathered, scribbling something onto that notepad of hers. Many times I'd been in her office in the past year and a half, wondering what kind of notes she was taking about me.

My last two semesters before graduating from FSU had been made up of exclusively online classes. After the news coverage of what happened with Joshua Caplan at my father's trial last year, I hated being out in public. The constant eyes on me, curious as to what I'd do next, took their toll and after speaking to my university's academic advisor, exceptions were made so that I could finish up my last year of school remotely in Miami.

The option of staying in my home city gave me the option of seeing a therapist regularly—Dr. Eloise, come highly recommended by my older sister, Monique. Every Monday at noon, I sat for an hour session where, from a brown leather chaise, I cut the front and got honest about my innermost feelings. If someone had informed me that someday I'd be at some shrink's office, talking about the contraindications of my childhood, I would have laughed my ass off.

But I made a promise.

It was a promise I could have easily broken, but when you bargain with the universe and the universe delivers, a little part of you *will* fear what may happen if you don't hold up your end of the deal. Last year, in Lauren's hospital room, I promised some unseen higher power that if she woke up in decent health, I would do something I didn't want to do in return.

Lauren ultimately did wake up, ultimately shutting me out over what could've only been a misunderstanding, but a promise was a promise.

So every Monday at noon, I watched Dr. Eloise scribble her notes after just about everything I'd say.

"I'm not dating the pop star," I revealed from where I laid. The scratching of her pen against paper could be heard, as she made a quiet sound that urged me to continue. "It's a publicity thing. She has her first American tour starting December 16th, and the more people payin' attention to her, the higher the likelihood they will see she's touring. Noise marketing. Tickets get sold."

"And this was…" Dr. Eloise's weathered brown eyes squinted to remember names. "…Marlon's idea?"

"Clearly."

She cracked a smile at my tone, scribbling something down. The gray of her curly 'fro flopped forward, slumping a stray curl along her forehead. The older woman was likely in her early sixties, a veteran therapist specializing in African-American focused mental health needs. Even though we'd likely come from very, very different backgrounds, there still remained an undercurrent of mutual understanding between the both of us.

She didn't cringe when I called my friends *"niggas"*, understood when I said certain things to be funny, and allowed me to leave my new persona as "Silas' replacement" at the door. The foundation of racial similarity that we started on, however flimsy, was worth something, at least.

"And what about law schools?" she pressed, bringing her note-taking pen between her teeth.

"I'm about to say something that makes me sound real ungrateful," I warned her.

She smiled, getting her ink ready. "Try me."

"I got into my first-choice school," I revealed, with an unexcited sigh. "They sent the acceptance in the mail earlier than I expected, offering up a whole care package to go with it—shirts, pens, folders, all of that."

Dr. Eloise, ever the professional, didn't scream her congratulations at me like just about everyone else. I was actually grateful for this. With a nod of her head, she simply issued a poised, "Congrats."

I nodded.

"So what's the problem?"

"I don't know if they accepted me because I actually earned it, or if it's because just about every law school in the country wants to be able to say they accepted the witness from that trial that went viral last summer."

A look of understanding crossed her features before quickly dissipating into her usual neutral expression. "Kain," she started as if gearing up to scold me, "remind me what your graduating GPA was again."

As much notes as Dr. Eloise took, I knew she wasn't asking because she didn't remember. She was asking so that I would be forced to speak my credentials out loud. I only looked at her, unwilling to blindly fall into this long practiced choreography of getting me to answer my own questions.

"It was perfect, if I'm not mistaken," she answered when met with my silence.

"Yeah," I confirmed.

"And your LSAT scores were very high as well, correct?"

"They were."

"Then you earned it, sir." My therapist shrugged as if this was more than obvious. "And when you show up for class next fall at Yale, you better act like it. But, somehow, I get the sense your apprehension has nothing to do with a question of qualification."

And this is why I pay her...

Dr. Eloise was very good at her job, exactly the kind of person I would recommend to those I cared about if I was the type of dude who went around suggesting therapists.

She leaned forward, giving me her undivided attention when she continued, "New Haven, Connecticut, is very far. Can we talk about your reservations about leaving Miami?"

"My reservations?"

"You haven't left the city for an extended period for about sixteen months. If I'm not mistaken, you also completed your last year of university online."

"But that's only because I never wanted to miss an appointment with you, doc."

Dr. Eloise chuckled, halfway rolling her eyes at that response. "Let's explore your unwillingness to leave, Kain. What's keeping you here?"

"It's a lot of things."

"Are you sure about that?" She was skeptical.

I got defensive. "Silas is locked up. If I leave, his whole operation goes to shit."

"You don't care about any of that," she said quietly.

This was the part of therapy that I hated the most—being told about myself by someone who purported themselves to somehow understand my decisions better than I did.

"Yes, I do."

Dr. Eloise rose from her seat, walking over to a filing cabinet and searching through it before pulling out a folder. When she returned to me, the folder opened to reveal a stack of handwritten notes in chronological order of date.

"Now that I've got my receipts—" I cracked a half-smile. "—let me ask you again. What's keeping you here, Kain?"

The truth remained frozen on my tongue, and that hollow feeling emerged yet again in the pit of my stomach.

"My family sits at the head of a billion-dollar drug ring, situated in the heart of Miami-Dade County, and if I leave, the business will suffer." Patient-doctor confidentiality is a beautiful thing. The elderly woman didn't even flinch, instead running an impatient hand through her gray short cut.

"That may be true, but—" Dr. Eloise pulled out a sheet of paper from her stack, and read "—on February 20th, 2017, you told me that if the whole empire crumbled tomorrow, you'd just have one less thing to stress about. Correct me if I'm wrong, but you don't sound like a person who cares if business suffers."

When I only shrugged, she continued to press harder.

"Is this about Lauren?"

"No."

This was an obvious lie, which my therapist picked up on quite easily. She carried on with her questioning as if I'd answered with a yes.

"Do you feel like if you leave for New Haven, you're only making the separation between the two of you stronger?"

"I have a legal document that says I can't get within 100 feet of her," I reminded. "The separation is damn strong."

Dr. Eloise cracked a smile and replied, "Your family sits at the head of a billion-dollar drug ring. Kain, there are men breaking the law on *your* orders as we speak. You expect me to believe you draw the line at breaking a restraining order?"

"It's not the law I'm respecting," I informed with a shake of my head. My therapist raised her eyebrows expectantly. "She wants me to keep my distance. If that's what she wants, then that's what I'll do."

When Lauren was in the hospital, I made her a promise as well. If she woke up, I promised to do whatever she wanted me to do. Even if that meant staying the fuck away from her.

"There's a small part of you that hopes she reaches out on her own. And that part of you is why you're wary about moving to New Haven. Am I right?"

I didn't answer the question, a habit of mine when questions with blaringly obvious answers are asked. Dr. Eloise continued, taking my silence as a yes.

"However, you know that she only filed the papers because she believes you betrayed her, yes?"

I nodded, knowing this to be true.

"Don't you think you'd get closure by telling her the truth?" Dr. Eloise didn't know the truth, either. The fact that Joshua Caplan was the person who shot Lauren was something I'd kept to myself for a year and a half. The only other people who knew the truth, besides me, was the person who'd helped me realize it, Vance, and, of course, the wrongly accused Silas.

"Telling the truth is easier said than done."

"Because?"

"I can't tell you," I told Dr. Eloise for what might've been the hundredth time since I started seeing her for sessions. I couldn't tell anyone. What Joshua Caplan had done to his daughter—regardless of it being an accident—was criminal. Dr. Eloise would not be bound by patient-doctor confidentiality if I gave her that kind of information. She would be legally obligated to report it.

And at the end of the day, the whole motivation for keeping the horrible truth to myself was for Lauren's sake. So I had to be careful about who I gave it out to. I could fix a lot of things, but I knew I wouldn't be able to fix whatever damage revealing the truth to Lauren would cause.

My therapist shut her folder full of notes, sensing that she was about to hit a wall with me. She was absolutely right.

"So what's the word on law school in New Haven?" She let that be her last question for me.

Chapter Seven

Lauren

"I had another dream about him last night," I confessed from the brown leather chaise situated in the center of my therapist's office.

Dr. Eloise raised a single eyebrow, a sympathetic look morphing into her aged face. "Who?"

I hated how she always made a point to make me say his name.

"Kain."

The word always sounded uncomfortable coming out of me in this office. For almost a year and a half now, since my shooting, I'd been seeing Dr. Eloise every Monday at four o'clock in the afternoon, pouring out the emotions I kept suppressed every other day. The fact that my parents were even forking over the money for me to see a therapist was the biggest plot twist. Before I was shot, my parents were never really huge proponents for things like therapy and mental health management. This was why they'd always scoffed at my desire to be a child psychiatrist.

I could've sworn that my father once held this age old, African-American belief that things like therapists were for fragile white people.

"What did you dream about?" Dr. Eloise questioned.

I drew in a shaky breath, closing my eyes as I laid back, trying to grasp at the fleeting memory of the dream. "I was sitting across from him in a pitch black room. Just two chairs and a spotlight overhead. We were sitting face-to-face and he was...*crying*."

"Was the reason clear?"

"Yes," I answered initially. "Well, not at first... He was very sad, though."

"And how did you feel?" Dr. Eloise questioned.

I opened one eye and snuck a look at her scratching fast notes into her notepad.

"I felt nothing," I admitted. "But... I mean, like... *super nothing*. I was sitting across from him, and all I could do was watch him suffer. I couldn't even feel my sense of self. It felt like I was watching us both from outside of my own body."

"And you just watched him cry," Dr. Eloise gathered as if this was nothing out of the ordinary.

"No." My eyes snapped open and I sat up to look at her. "You don't understand—Kain *doesn't* cry. Like, ever."

Dr. Eloise only nodded at this information, scribbling something down. "So, did he say why he was sad?"

"He was sad because I lost the baby," I replied. She stopped scribbling, her eyes rising from her notepad with a sympathetic softness. I took handfuls of my hair as I tried to make sense of the dream from where I sat. "He told me he wasn't mad at me for not telling him, and then admitted to wanting a family. It broke his heart that I'd lost the baby. He was totally unraveling over it. It was so... I don't know."

"It was so what?" she pressed.

"*Real...*"

"Real like the others?"

I nodded. This wasn't the first dream about Kain that I'd had that played out in this way.

"But is it possible to dream about something I've never seen before? I've never seen Kain cry before, Dr. Eloise."

"It's possible," she replied. "So what do you think the dream means?"

I wracked my brain for an answer, ultimately giving up because I didn't have any idea.

"I think I'm just jealous that he's dating Eden Xavier," I admitted.

"I see." I always felt like Dr. Eloise knew things about me that I hadn't told her when she'd hit me with those short responses. "Three months ago, you told me you were over him."

"I'm supposed to be, right?"

"That's your call, Lauren."

"Well *I am* supposed to be." I crossed my arms, hating how deep down, I didn't believe in what I was saying. "His father tried to kill me, and he got on the stand and defended him. To make things worse, he ruined my father's law career in the process."

"Are you reminding me, Lauren? Or are you reminding yoursel—"

"I don't know!"

"Lauren," Dr. Eloise spoke in soothing tones, trying to calm me down. I drew in a long breath, and made a show of exhaling slowly, trying to give off at least the appearance of checking myself.

"I'm sorry for shouting at you." She accepted my apology with a nod. "It's just… Okay, so he took her to *my* favorite restaurant. That's where we had our first date and everything." I caught my voice cracking.

"And how does that make you feel?" my therapist pressed for details.

"Angry."

"Why?"

"Because…"

"I need a better answer from you, Lauren," she encouraged.

"Angry—just angry. I don't know why. Just angry." I raked my fingers through my hair, frustrated. "She looks *nothing* like me, by the way. All the others he was seen with—they looked like me."

"And that made you feel good," she guessed.

"It made me feel like he still thought about me, yes."

"And that's important to you."

I nodded, a little ashamed that this was my truth. Dr. Eloise offered me a faint smile, pleased that she was getting real answers out of me. "So this dream," she came back to my original point. "You never got the chance to discuss the miscarriage with him in real life, correct?"

"I never even told him I was pregnant."

"Do you feel like you're denying yourself a chance at healing by never having this conversation?"

I squinted. "Doctor, you don't get it. He. Defended. The. Man. Who. Tried. To. Kill. Me. It's not like I can just show up at his doorstep, and be like, '*Let's have a conversation, Kainie.*' I can't even see a picture of him without getting so... *mad.*"

"Let's unpack that. What are you most angry about?"

"He lied to me."

"About?"

"He said he loved me. He got me to open up to him in every way, and then he just... Ugh! It pisses me off every time I think about it."

"And yet you still have feelings for him," she guessed. I was annoyed now. Just because something is true, doesn't mean it needs to be said.

"I read online that as a woman, I will always feel *something* for the person who took my innocence."

Dr. Eloise raised a vaguely skeptical brow. "Me and about a dozen of my friends must be exceptions to this rule, then."

"I'm sure when I'm your age, I won't feel anything for Kain either." She made a face before chuckling to herself. "No offense," I added.

"If you want to wait forty years to get over an ex, that's your prerogative, Ms. Caplan."

I shivered at the thought. "I don't want to talk about Kain anymore," I announced.

"That's fine. What else would you like to discuss?"

For a moment, I only sat there. Finally, I cleared my throat, drawing in an easing breath before I said the words, "Rashad forced himself on me last Thursday."

* * *

My parents always smiled so damn hard whenever Rashad came over for dinner. If not for Rashad, I might've never known what it looked like when my parents approved of my boyfriend.

Dr. Eloise, with her encouragements to cut Rashad loose, didn't realize how important that was for me. After months of feeling like my parents secretly hated me, bringing Rashad around made them act different. Their smiles were for him, but sometimes I could fool myself into feeling like while they smiled for him, they were silently happy with me for having brought him home.

Rashad, my *Beauvais*-approved boyfriend, complete with a legally-earned trust fund, good Creole genes, and a lifelong membership to the same fraternity my father was in.

My parents were no doubt already planning our wedding.

We sat at the dinner table, eating as Dad and Rashad talked politics. Lately, my boyfriend had taken to calling my father Governor Caplan. *Ugh, he was so annoying*... Dad pretended to be embarrassed by the title, but I noted how he didn't actually discourage Rashad at all—especially since he readily answered to it.

"Governor Caplan."

"Yeah, son."

I didn't know which pet name made me cringe the most—Governor Caplan or son. I tuned out their conversation until I heard myself being talked about.

"Our girl is turning twenty-one in just a few weeks," Dad reminded. I hated that my father felt the need to remind my boyfriend that my birthday was coming up. My birthday was December sixteenth, which was fifteen days away on a Saturday. Rashad had more than enough time to remember it on his own.

As a joke, Rashad turned his head toward Morgan and wished her a happy early birthday. My parents seemed to find this just hilarious. I cracked a smile, not wanting to be a mood kill, but I was not amused. Morgan snuck a knowing glance at me, and from the look on her face, I knew she didn't think Rashad's joke was all that amusing either.

"Any big plans?" my father asked Rashad.

If anyone had asked me, I would've said it felt like my father was trying to silently communicate that if Rashad wanted my hand in marriage, all he'd need to do was ask. My father may have said the words, '*Any big plans?*', but I heard the words, '*You have my blessing if you want her.*'

"I was going to surprise her on the night of, but since everyone is curious," Rashad started, ready to ruin my birthday surprise to appease my father. He took out his phone and pulled up something on the screen before handing it to me. The bright backlight of his cell burned into my irises, a single name displayed in big, bold, and green font.

Eden Xavier

"I got us floor seat tickets to her first ever concert and the after party," Rashad informed as I read the ticket details off the screen, her name in a bright, flashing green beside an e-receipt for two VIP tickets that evidently set Rashad back almost eight hundred dollars to buy.

I wondered if I would look ungrateful if I asked him if it was too late to get his money back. Whatever I was feeling in the base of my stomach must've showed itself prominently on my face because the excitement in Rashad's eyes faded.

"You don't like it," he guessed, his tone halfway between disappointed and... *angry?*

I suddenly felt like everyone at the table decided to give me their undivided attention. I snuck a glance at my parents who looked to be holding their breath, quietly hoping they hadn't raised me to be the kind of daughter who would turn her nose up at a polite gesture. The longer I stayed quiet, the deeper the crease between my father's eyes grew.

"No, I love it," I broke the quiet, pushing out a dejected sigh. The atmosphere around me that seemed to halt for my response came alive again. My parents commended my boyfriend on such a thoughtful gift, and he readily accepted their praise. It was Morgan, whose dark brown eyes found me amidst the commotion at the table, that gave me yet another knowing look for the second time tonight. I could sense an oncoming conversation between the both of us once we got some privacy.

"Lauren loves that one song by her," my mother assured, turning her attention to my sister. "Momo, how does it go?"

"I'm not so sure Lauren loves that song *anymore*," Morgan replied to our mother, shaking her head with a wry chuckle. As a dumbfounded look settled into our mother's features, I moved my hand to cover my mouth, hiding the slight smile that threatened to come out. Morgan shot me a wink, unwilling to hide her own smirk.

Rashad looked from me to Morgan, belting out a not so genuine giggle. "You two got a secret twin language, or some?"

Even though he was smiling, I could tell Rashad was less than comfortable with the possibility that Morgan and I might be non-verbally communicating about him. Morgan shrugged her shoulders, looking at him as if he was a fly, invading her space. She let him squirm under her analytical gaze before she finally responded.

"Yeah, we do." My sister looked at me with a tilt of her head, silently informing me that if I had any reservations about going to the concert, now was my moment to speak up. I bit my lower lip nervously and looked down at my half-eaten dinner. When she realized I wasn't going to seize the opportunity, she pushed out a sigh and said to Rashad, "I'm sure you two will have a blast."

* * *

Morgan sat at the foot of my bed, watching me as I French braided the other half of my head at my vanity. In the reflection coming off my mirror, her eyes met mine for an extended moment of silence, and I could tell from the way she drew in one long breath that she was getting ready to lecture me.

"Why are you still with that clown?"

This wasn't the first time someone had questioned my decision to be with Rashad today. After I'd explained the sequence of events that ultimately lead to me buying *Plan B* emergency contraceptive at an out-of-town *Walgreens*, Dr. Eloise had asked a similar question with a tone identical to my sister's voice now.

"I don't know what you mean." I skirted around the topic, no longer meeting my sister's eyes in the mirror. In the several months that had followed my shooting, while it seemed like everything around me was crumbling, my relationship with my sister had only gotten stronger.

My almost dying had an interesting way of putting things into perspective for her. The relationship I had with my parents may have been changed beyond repair, but Morgan and I had never been closer.

"You don't even like him," Morgan stressed.

"I never said that."

"You don't have to!" She stood to her feet and walked up closer behind me. "Every time he opens his mouth, you look like you want to shoot yourself in the face."

"No, I don't," I disagreed.

"Look at me," Morgan ordered, trying her best to look as tortured as possible. "That's what you look like when he talks."

I bit back a smile over her theatrics.

"Lauren!" she stressed. "Nobody is laughing. *Why* are you with that clown?"

With a shake of my head, I attempted to dismiss her opinions. "I like him, Morgan."

"You like him the same way I like a migraine." After making a grand show of rolling her eyes slowly, she muttered, "He's not your type."

"I don't have a type."

"Yes, you do."

"What's my type, then?"

"I don't know, but it's not Rashad. Shit, Rashad is more Dad's type than anything—" Morgan stopped talking abruptly, having found the answer to her question on her own. "You think dating a twenty-six year old man who calls our father '*Governor Caplan*' unironically is what you need to do to be Daddy's favorite again?"

"I'm not trying to be Daddy's favorite," I muttered. *I just want him to seem like he's happy to see me from time to time.*

My father had been behaving strangely around me ever since I came out of the hospital. If he even bothered to acknowledge that I was in the room, he hardly ever looked me square in the eye. Rarely did it ever seem like my father even wanted to be in the same room as me; forget holding a conversation longer than five minutes with me.

"Lauren..." Morgan rested two hands on either of my shoulders, staring at my face in the mirror's reflection. She stood above my head, her eyes falling to me sympathetically. "Take it from someone who never really connected with Daddy in the first place... Our dad is not worth this much effort."

How could she say that?

"I didn't know you felt that way."

Morgan squinted. "Really?"

"Yeah."

"Before you linked up with Thug Bae—" I cringed "—you never noticed that Daddy and I didn't really talk... like, ever?"

"Well, yeah, but—"

"Daddy was never really trying to hear what I was saying. I wasn't as polite as you. My grades weren't as high as yours. He couldn't brag about me the way he could brag about you. You were his favorite."

"Well, you were *Mom's* favorite."

"Lauren, please." Morgan rolled her eyes. "Mom felt *sorry* for me. She gave me the attention Daddy was too busy giving you so I wouldn't feel left out. But it's not like Mom ignored you. I'm telling you—Daddy used to not even see me if you were in the room."

My mind wandered to dozens of memories I had of Daddy not-so-discretely letting me know he preferred me over my sister. Although, it never used to raise red flags because I'd always written it off as me being for Dad and Morgan being for Mom. However, if I really thought on it, the fact that Mom had a slightly stronger bond with Morgan didn't really make her behavior towards me noticeably different. The same, however, couldn't be said for our father towards Morgan.

Almost as soon as I made that connection, the years of hostility Morgan dished out towards me made sense. The past year of our improving relationship, while my relationship with our father struggled, finally made sense as well.

"And now the roles are switched," I offered. "Now Daddy's all about you."

Morgan shook her head. "Daddy is all about whatever makes him look good at any point in time. Right now, that's me because of your mess with Thug Bae—" *cringe* "—last year. But you can't erase several years of blatant favoritism overnight, Lori. Our father is such a..."

"...politician," I finished her sentence.

She chuckled at this, nodding her head. "Sure, let's go with that."

"How come you never talked to me about all of this before?"

My sister's cheek turned up in a subtle half smile, sad in color. "Because it's one of those things you have to go through to actually understand. If I walked up to Lauren two years ago and said, '*Daddy is kind of cold and unloving*,' she would have rolled her eyes and said I wasn't trying hard enough to connect with him."

I nodded, knowing that is precisely what I would've said.

"But now you know," Morgan sighed. "I mean, look at you, dating some corny weirdo just so Daddy will know how devoted you are to keeping up appearances. You get it now…" She shook her head and repeated, "You get it now."

Chapter Eight

KAIN

Javier Perez had untrustworthy energy.

And I didn't feel that way just because he was a politician. I was raised on the ability to scan a sea of faces and easily pick out the most disloyal in the bunch. Javier Perez had one of those vibes—features pinched and twisted, like once upon a time he's smelled something bad and never got around to fixing his face.

He leaned forward and took another sip from his glass of whiskey. He'd been sipping on that drink for the better part of the last half-hour. I didn't know it before I saw it, but I didn't like that shit. It looked suspicious.

"That liquor's expensive. Don't just sit around and let your ice water it down—drink it. That's my money in that glass."

The moment I let the words come out of my mouth, the quiet tension of the room grew hostile. The armed guards behind the Cuban candidate drew in as if getting ready to make me apologize for my less than respectful outburst.

Javier tossed a look to his security personnel, raising a hand for them to stand down. My left cheek rose with a smirk before I snuck a look at the watch on my wrist. It was a quarter till midnight, so that meant that Mr. Perez and his peeps had fifteen minutes of my time left.

"Loo-look, Kain," Javier stuttered, his eye contact unstable. "The city council had an understanding with your father when he was free."

"Well, he ain't free no more."

"Silas always made sure to endorse anyone we pushed for political office. He was a man of great influence in this state, and now that he's..." he hesitated. "...unable, we feel that an endorsement from you is just what it would take to give my run for governor the push it needs."

Javier would need more than just a push.

He would need thousands of early voter ballots, paid for and pulled from the black and brown hands of Miami-Dade's poorest neighborhoods. No politician could outright set aside campaign money to fund ballot fraud, so that's where Silas' "influence" and "endorsement" always came in handy. Using his own money, my father used to buy the ballots, propping up whichever candidate offered him the best incentives.

Crooked politicians like Javier Perez were the backbone of my father's entire organization.

"If elected governor, I would do everything in my power to see that your father's upcoming trial for shooting that girl is thrown out."

This, apparently was the best incentive that Perez had to offer. Clearly, I wasn't sold.

"It's a win-win situation," he tried to convince me.

Debatable.

"Really?" I reached for my cellphone on the table between us, checking to see if I had any messages and for how much time Javier had left. "Everything I've heard so far tips the scale in your favor. I don't do favors, Javier; I trade."

Truth is, he was gonna have to offer me a hell of a lot more for me to consider doing what he asked of me. He get's to be governor of one of the most populous states in the country, and I got what exactly? My father back?

Who says I wanted him back?

Neither of us spoke for an extended period of time, making it easier to hear the buzzing noise coming up from downstairs. Below our feet, the vibrations of the hottest party in Miami buzzed beneath us, an after party celebrating the successful completion of Eden Xavier's first ever concert.

The label was using the biggest club that I owned as a venue, a warehouse-sized nightclub called *Seven* in the Miami neighborhood of Wynwood. I sat in on this impromptu meeting with Javier while the party raged on beneath my feet in my soundproofed, second floor office.

"Once I get the governor's seat—"

"*If* you get the governor's seat."

Javier shifted uncomfortably in his seat, correcting himself. "If I was elected governor of the state, that would mean decreased police presence in the neighborhoods where you and your people operate. Less spontaneous raids in your clubs and other establishments. A win for me, is a win for you financially. You'll certainly be sleeping easier."

"A loss for you — still a win for me financially, as far as I'm concerned." I checked my watch again. Only three minutes had passed. My eyes shot up from my watch, just in time to catch Javier sipping at his watered down whisky again. "And I'm sleepin' just fine."

"Not with Caplan as governor," Javier quipped. "The man has had it out for your family since he was the state's attorney. While I would try to make your life easier, he would do everything he can to bring the Montgomery name down."

While true, it still wasn't enough of an argument to convince me to help this shifty-eyed man. While it might've been Silas' prerogative to help out anyone who promised him a kickback, I wasn't so forthcoming. Regardless of whether or not we had an ally in the governor's seat, my family would be just fine. Javier was going to have to try harder than that to convince me of anything.

My hatred for Joshua Caplan would've been all the motivation I needed had I been able to find anything about Perez that I trusted.

"I can handle Caplan. So I don't believe I really need to help put you in office," I informed. Javier's gaze fell pathetically. That was it for me. "What are you — thirty-seven?" Fifteen years older than myself. Javier confirmed the valuation with a nod. "You are way too damn old to not be lookin' niggas in the eye when you're tryna have a one-to-one, askin' them for things."

I bet Caplan is tearing his ass up in debates.

"Look, I came to you with something to offer." He put a little more bass in his voice. That whiskey was clearly kicking in. "A favor for a favor—"

"A favor for an I-O-U," I clarified. "You ain't offered me shit, but promises for *after* you already get what you want."

"Kain—"

"Mr. Montgomery."

"Mr. Montgomery—" If I got nothing else from taking this meeting, at least I got a laugh. "—I just figured considering your history with the family, you would also see it as a benefit to have someone else as governor. You can help in many ways, too. After the whole fiasco with his daughter last year, I bet you have a lot of dirt on—"

No longer amused, I lunged out of my seat, my hands grabbing Javier by the front of his suit before he could even finish that sentence. The audible sounds of his security guards cocking the guns they'd snuck into the club echoed, and I threatened, "Tell 'em to shoot, and even if they miss, see if you make it out of this club with your head on your shoulders."

"*Cálmese,*" Javier barked in Spanish to his men. "*Está bien!*"

They froze behind their boss, but my grip on the collar of his shirt did not let up as I warned, "If her name shows up in anything that your campaign draws up against Caplan... If you even allude to her, even if it has nothing to do with me, you're gonna need more than two niggas with Glocks to stop what you got comin'. I don't care what you say about Caplan, but you be sure to keep his daughter's name out the papers, or else you'll have to answer to me."

This was the threat I'd been levying against every governor-hopeful that I'd seen in the past five months, each of them hoping that my past relationship with Lauren Caplan was fair game to use against her father's run for office. In threatening them to keep Lauren out it, I knew I was indirectly helping Caplan's campaign by making his rivals too afraid to use their biggest criticism against him, but I had to look out for her. If Lauren's past relationship with me was used by any of her father's rivals, I just knew it would be something held against her in the toxic environment that was her household.

In the months since Caplan had announced his candidacy, it didn't escape my notice that Lauren was barely ever present for his public appearances. It was obvious he was hiding her because he was wary about the public being reminded of her past. That observation alone is what had me promising random politicians from all around the state that I'd kill them if they even thought about talking about her.

Every time I caught myself doing it, I was met with the reality that I was just as protective of Lauren as I was sixteen months ago. A realization that never failed to put me in an incredibly bad mood. With a fistful of Javier Perez's shirt still in my hands, I checked the time on my watch one last time.

"Your fifteen minutes are up." It was midnight.

* * *

Lauren

As soon as the clock struck twelve, Rashad's drunk ass started to sing.

"*Happy buuuuuuurthday to you. Happy buuuuuuuuuuuuuuuuuurthday to you.*"

He'd been drinking for the entirety of our evening—three shots before the stupid concert, a whole flask that he'd snuck in to the stupid concert, and now that we were in line outside of a nightclub called *Seven*, trying to get into the stupid concert's afterparty, he was totally wasted.

"Baby, baby, baby..." he half shouted, half whispered, taking my face between his clammy hands. "You look so, so good tonight."

"Don't call me that," I squirmed from under his sweaty hands. His face morphed into a frown, annoyed that even as he gave me compliments, all I could do was cringe at the sound of him calling me "*baby*". He would've much preferred I act modest and shower him in gratitude for acknowledging that, yes, I was a pretty girl.

But I already knew that I looked good.

And I didn't need the opinion of a drunk man to confirm the fact.

Rashad waited until we were nodded into the party by a bouncer before he said anything else to me. Under the multicolored LED lights of the crowded party, he grabbed at my shoulders, forcing me to look at him.

"You think you're too good for me?" he questioned, clearly getting brave off the countless drinks he'd gulped down that evening. "No, really, Lauren. Is that what you think?"

He pushed me into a quieter corner of the club, his movements sloppy, under the influence. The sounds of music were muffled in the hallway leading to the bathrooms that he'd dragged me to.

"I never said that."

"You don't have to," Rashad retorted. "I can see it in the high and mighty act you put up every time I try to say something nice to you. If I call you beautiful, you're supposed to say thank you. Not twist your face like some *uptight bitch* over the fact that I called you baby. "

"Thank you for the compliment," I tried to talk down the storm I felt brewing. But from the way Rashad's face was set, I knew it was too late to stop what had already started. He wanted to have this fight, so that's what we were going to do.

"No!" he said. "Don't be fake now. You really think you're Morgan, huh?"

I just blinked, not exactly offended, but merely taken aback.

"You think you're some type of debutante? You really think respectable niggas are lining up at the door trying to wife you up?" He laughed a little to himself. "You forget you was out here poppin' your pussy for a nigga who should be put under the jail."

Alcohol makes people so ugly.

At the sound of his last statement, I turned to put some distance between Rashad and myself. I was not going to stand there and listen to him insult me in his drunken rage. The minute I turned my head, his hands roughly gripped at my shoulders, forcing me to face him as he continued with his vitriolic rant.

"Nobody out here is trying to put their last name on a thug's whore. Tell your Daddy that. He's making me sick every time he fixes his mouth to call me his son." I absorbed each and every word like it was nothing. This wouldn't be the first time Rashad got drunk and told me how he really felt about me. Tomorrow, he would wake up, realize he couldn't do any better, and then spend the rest of the day sending me five hundred-word apology text messages. "You can be the most beautiful woman in the world, but every man who learns your story will always see you as one thing first—trash. Tainted goods."

* * *

When I sat down at the stocked bar amidst the commotion, I did so with every intention of taking advantage of the free alcohol that came with the purchase of entry into Eden Xavier's afterparty.

"Can I see your ID?" the bartender behind the counter questioned when I asked for a vodka cranberry. For a moment, disappointment settled into my chest before I remembered that it was long after midnight, meaning it was officially my twenty-first birthday. I could get this drink legally.

Setting my purse on the counter, I pulled out my wallet.

After the bartender read my birthday off my driver's license, he broke into a smile. "Well, you certainly didn't waste any time."

"Vodka cranberry," I repeated my order to the man behind the counter. His smile faded slightly into a grimace over my demanding tone, but he brought it right back. Candidly speaking, he was an attractive man, standing about two or three inches above my head, with deep brown skin, brown eyes, and a shining smile. I assessed him shamelessly. Under the mood lighting of the nightclub, colored bulbs reflected back in his eyes as he looked me over just as openly.

Appearance wise, this man was more my taste, but I had a strict list of things I looked for in a man these days, and Mr. Bartender here was way too reminiscent of the type of men I'd sworn off. He was fun to look at, however.

"How you in such a sour mood on your birthday?" he asked, making no moves to get me what I was asking for. In fact, if I wasn't mistaken, his tone took on a flirtatious color. "And no, ma. Vodka cranberry ain't the drink you want to be your first. Let me get you something special."

"This isn't my first drink." *Not by a long shot...*

"It's your first legal drink, ain't it?"

Around us, house remixes of Eden's songs blared through surround sound speakers. She was nowhere to be seen, however, likely still recuperating from what was objectively a great first concert. I still didn't like her, but I had to give credit where it was due. Good music was good music. The man I'd come here with was off somewhere on the dance floor, awkwardly flailing about, probably thinking he was making me jealous.

He wasn't.

I just really needed this drink. Calmly, I tried to express this to the bartender who was so hellbent on making small talk. He met my quiet request with a smile.

"A birthday this important needs an equally important drink," he announced, pulling out a round glass bottle from under the counter. "This stuff isn't for sale. It actually is part of the club owner's personal stash, but I won't tell if you don't."

Since this was Miami, the club owner could have only been one person. I didn't make any sudden movements, keeping my cool as the young man in front of me reached behind for a shot glass.

"This stuff's expensive," he informed, pushing the bottle up so that I could read it. *L'Essence de Courvoisie*, I read off the beautifully shaped glass bottle, filled halfway with brown liquor. "It's cognac. Is that alright with you?"

"I don't care," I replied honestly. I just needed a drink.

"I got you." He poured the liquor just shy of the shot glass brim, his eyes peering up to see if I felt threatened by the amount he'd given me. I had to stop myself from rolling my eyes. "There you go, Lauren."

I squinted at his usage of my name. Did I know him from somewhere?

In response to my reaction, he explained, "I read your name off your driver's license. I'm Josiah, by the way. But the ladies call me Joey, so feel free."

I only chuckled, reaching for the glass in front of me. In one swift motion, I downed the entire drink.

"Whoa, whoa, whoa," Josiah raised an outraged hand. "No, you can't toss that back like it's some cheap shot of Everclear. This cognac costs three thousand dollars. You have to savor it."

"Oops."

He reached for my glass and poured me another. "Try again."

This time I was a little more deliberate with my sip, watching the man behind the counter cautiously as he nodded in approval.

"Did you say that this whole bottle was three grand?" I questioned after setting my glass down. "Can't you get in trouble for just taking it upon yourself to just give it out like this for free?"

"It's just two drinks," he assured, but then he seemed to decide it was best to quit while we were ahead. "Let me make you that vodka cranberry now."

"Wait." I stopped him. "Would you by any chance have a cheaper version of this drink?"

Josiah cracked a smile. "Cognac? For sure, pretty lady. *Remy* or *Hennessy*?"

"Whichever one gets me drunk the fastest."

"So what's your story?" he asked as he poured me my sixth shot. "What's a pretty girl like you doing alone at a nightclub's bar on her birthday?"

My glass vibrated against the brown, wooden bar counter, moving slightly to the bass of the music that blasted throughout the club. I reached for it, turning my chin up to look at Josiah when I replied. "I'm not here alone. I came with my boyfriend."

"Then where he at?"

I didn't reply right away, choosing to take a quick gulp before pushing my glass forward for another shot. "Who cares."

"Ooh," he forced a wince, clutching his heart as if it broke for me. "Is that why you're on your seventh shot of brown?"

I didn't acknowledge the question until he poured it for me. "Yeah, probably."

I forced down the drink quickly.

"You might wanna let up on all that *Henny*, though. It sneaks up on you."

"One more shot," I urged, coaxing him for an eighth.

"You too small to be going through eight shots of cognac in less than thirty minutes."

"Do I look drunk to you?" I raised my eyebrows, my face the picture of sobriety. Over the past few months, in the days when I'd numbed myself with alcohol to drown out the memories that summer, I'd developed quite an impressive tolerance. Sure, my drink of choice had usually been wine, but the brown liquor coursing through my veins at the moment didn't feel any different than usual. I just needed to get my mind off of things. Tonight wasn't the first time Rashad had exploded on me, but that didn't make the harsh words he'd dished out any easier to carry. Just because I didn't cry, didn't mean his words didn't weigh on me. "Just one more."

"Last one," Josiah gave in, pouring me an eighth shot. I eyed the drink in the cup, noting the rising heat in my face that told me my oncoming buzz was close. Without much time set aside for processing, I downed the eighth drink. I could feel myself getting numb, and a small part of me realized it probably wasn't the best decision to have had all these drinks on an empty stomach. "Now let's hear your story, pretty girl."

Cracking a hazy smile, I questioned, "Is that what you do? You pick a girl, pump her full of drinks, and then pry into her personal life?"

Josiah leaned against the counter, arms resting on the surface, drawing closer to my face in the midst of the commotion of the party. "Only when I'm curious. Only when she's fine as hell. I'm just trying to see what's up with it."

He rose a suggestive eyebrow.

"I don't think my man would appreciate seeing you so close to my face right now," I informed.

His features twisted into a dreamy-eyed smirk, his gaze brushing over my face and body hungrily before ultimately coming back to meet my eyes. "He left you by yourself, looking the way you look, on your birthday. Believe me..." His smile grew, an air of cockiness about it, "...your man should've expected this."

"So, I guess I'm just for everybody, huh?" My voice was quiet, and I was no longer passing my words through a filter on account of the liquor starting to take effect in my system. Josiah's smile faded, his eyes widening at my interpretation of his behavior. "Just some cheap Miami jumpoff, caught within some strange gray area between respectable and whore. I have a boyfriend, I say. It doesn't matter, you essentially reply." I laughed humorlessly, whispering, "What do you take me for?"

He rushed into an excuse. "I didn't mean to disrespect—"

"What is it about me?" I asked, interrupting him. My alcohol-induced brashness was unrelenting, my insecurities emerging prominently. "Is it etched into my body with invisible ink? Or do I just give off some unseen vibe now? Do I look like I get down like that? You're at work, man. Where's your sense of professionalism? Am I not good enough to get some semblance of decency? Why do men think they can just *have* me? I'm a *person*, not a toy. You can't *have* me..."

Memories of Rashad on my back, pushing me into the softness of his mattress, using my body as if it were disposable, flashed in broken segments through my mind. The three week-old memory was just as vivid as if it occurred yesterday. I closed my eyes hard, bringing my hands to my head as the room began to spin. Tears slipped out from the tight shut of my eyelids.

"Look." I could feel Josiah drawing back, creating some distance. "That *Hennessy* is clearly creeping in on you. It's really not that deep, I was just trying to have a conversation."

Men always mistake the youthfulness of my features for naiveté. Like I don't know lust when I see it. Like I don't know what it looks like when a man looks at you like you're only good for one thing. Men are so gross, so insufferable. Trash, they're trash.

"Here's a glass of water. Drink it, and sober up some, ma."

I hopped off the bar stool I was seated on, wiping at my cheeks. Without taking the glass of water offered, I slipped into a crowd of dancing partygoers, my eyes scanning the crowd for Rashad. I was ready to go home.

It didn't take long for me to find his ultra fair-skinned complexion in the sea of black and brown bodies on the floor, dancing with some red bodycon-clad stranger. He danced with all his energy, beads of sweat forming at his hair line and clumping together the sandy brown curls that hung over his forehead.

I cut in between them, my balance a little wobbly when I turned to face my boyfriend.

"Shad, I want to go home," I shouted over the music.

He was still dancing, half listening to me in his drunken, adrenaline-boosted state. His response came so slow that for a second, I thought he might be ignoring me.

"We just got here." There was no room for negotiation in his dismissive delivery, in the way his hand wrapped around my shoulder and moved me out of the way so he could continue to dance with his new friend.

"*I want to go home!*" I screamed even louder, briefly calling the attention of some of the people that surrounded us. I was ready to make a scene as the alcohol within me cut away my self-control. Rashad turned to face me, expression set in a irritated scowl, his eyes bouncing about over my head, no doubt meeting the stares of onlookers.

"So *go*, Lauren." He nodded for me to get gone. "I'm staying, though. I paid big money to be at this party."

Rashad's wild eyes stared into me, willing me to make myself scarce so he could freely enjoy himself. Clearly I was killing his vibe, and he really wanted me to leave. The fact that it was my birthday seemed to mean nothing to him as he turned his attention away from me, getting right back to the good time he was trying to have.

I didn't know if the alcohol was making me emotional, but I felt pins and needles in the backs of my eyes. Usually, it didn't bother me when Rashad behaved this way. As my sister Morgan had stated many nights before, I didn't even like Rashad, so him treating me like this didn't exactly break my heart. However, the liquor coursing through my system made it much harder to keep myself together like I usually did. I wasn't crying because Rashad was treating me poorly.

I was crying because this was my life now.

I was crying because I already knew that when Rashad texted me whatever five hundred-word apology letter about his behavior tomorrow, I was going to just accept it. And then the cycle would begin again—Rashad ripping into my self-worth, and me taking him back every time because neither of us could do any better.

Tucked away in an empty hallway of the nightclub, I leaned back against a wall, willing the space around me to stop spinning. Even though I was standing still on solid ground, I somehow felt the nausea of motion sickness. I couldn't find my purse, and in my dizzying state, I couldn't seem to retrace my steps for where I might've set it down. My phone was in my purse, leaving me unable to call myself an Uber back home.

I tried to take control of my breathing, walking in zig-zags along a dimly lit corridor, looking for an exit. Every odd second, I swallowed back a dry heave, trying to keep the hot rumbling in my stomach from climbing up my throat.

Hennessy—never again.

I reached the end of the hallway, finding not a door, but a black metal spiral staircase. Knowing I didn't want to walk back to the sea of people I'd rushed away from in the main club, I grabbed hold of the cold iron railing. I followed each rising step up to a solid black door, and I twisted the handle once, hoping it would lead to some sort of fire escape.

It was locked.

With a disappointed sigh, I pressed my forehead onto the metal door, banging my head against the surface softly while inwardly coaching my drunk ass on how I was going to safely make it down those stairs, make my way through the dense crowd, and leave through the front entrance.

Drawing in a preparatory breath, I eased myself straight, using the closed entryway in front of me as support, and released a calming exhale.

An audible click resonated from the door, the sound of unlocking. There was barely enough time to register what was happening, especially not when my liquored up condition made the world around me move discontinuously. The door disappeared from under my hands. My feet remained planted where they were, as the door in front of me swung inward, and it felt like everything in me dropped when the person at the other end came into view.

Kain.

Kain Tariq Montgomery.

Sixteen months later.

Unconsciously, I took two shaky steps back, seemingly forgetting that behind me was a winding staircase and a long way down. Just before my third step, his hand came up automatically, catching me at my waist before I could even begin to fall backward.

Neither of us said anything as I stood there, dumbfounded by the gravity of being in his presence for the first time in over a year. Wordlessly, he pulled me away from the staircase's edge, his hand slipping from my side. I was too drunk to focus on the intricate details about him that had changed, but not drunk enough to have missed the fact that several things about his appearance were different now.

One thing remained constant, however.

As always, Kain was a fortress when he wanted to be, giving away nothing in terms of facial expression or readable emotions. Sure, he was looking at me, but nothing in his face gave away even a hint of what he might've been thinking.

For the umpteenth time that night, the hot rumbling of nausea climbed up my digestive system again. Caught up within the unexpectedness of standing before Kain Montgomery, of all people, I was slow to swallow it down. Halfway up my throat, there was nothing I could do to stop the eight shots I'd forced down that night from coming back up.

All over Kain Montgomery's crisp, white dress shirt.

Chapter Nine

KAIN

My shirt smelled like *Hennessy*.

This realization elicited a chuckle out of me because just because it was legal, didn't mean that was the drink for her. It was a little after one o'clock in the morning, December 16th, 2017. If my memory served correctly, a girl I hadn't seen since she was nineteen, was now twenty-one. The law said Lauren could finally drink whichever spirit she so pleased, but Lauren… Lauren was definitely more of a wine person.

She was drunk. Drunk off her ass, actually, growing more intoxicated by the minute as the slow progression of the liquor she'd ingested worked its way through her bloodstream. *Hennessy—which one of those dumbass niggas downstairs gave her skinny self Hennessy*?

"I don't want to… don't want to go inside… with you," she complained in fragments as I shut the door behind us. It hadn't been my intention to pull her into the second floor office, but one look over the state of her, and I had to make a quick decision.

I couldn't let her leave—not like this.

Her balance was a little unstable, her steps uncertain as I ushered her to the couches in the center of the room. The second floor office above *Seven* was a large space, furnished like a makeshift studio apartment for the sake of convenience. When I was growing up, my father always used to tell me a real man is always prepared for any outcome. Because of this, in just about every nightclub my family owned, an office that could double as a living space was never too far off.

Once Lauren was safely planted in a seat, I made my way to the other side of the room, my hands automatically moving to the buttons on my soiled shirt. Peeling off the wet undershirt I had on as well, I opened the office's closet door and grabbed a towel first, wiping off the cognac-scented droplets that remained on my skin. As I wiped myself down, it didn't escape my notice that I couldn't imagine myself tolerating this shit in any other situation.

Where did all this patience come from?

I pulled a clean white t-shirt over my head, looking over my shoulder in Lauren's direction once I'd changed out of the dirtied clothes. Like a thief caught red-handed, her head snapped away, looking on elsewhere.

Before I said anything, I took a moment to look over her, making note of the things about her that weren't the same anymore. She'd lost a bit of weight, not just thin in the places where she used to be thicker, but all over. The once sienna brown tone of her skin, which I looked for in every woman I looked twice at after her, took on a bronzer shade now, a sign that she probably spent most of her days indoors. I noted the way that she kept her entire body turned away from where I stood, refusing to even breathe in my direction.

Her childish, drunk ass...

I cracked a smile. Despite the critical differences from the one I remembered, this was no doubt Lauren. In the flesh, for the first time in sixteen months. I leaned my shoulder against the closed closet door beside me, using this moment to silently look at her, take it all in.

She was still beautiful.

Despite the changes in her appearance, she was still beautiful. Lauren wouldn't look my way, her silence in the room somehow taking up space. When her head ultimately drooped forward, I straightened up, walking to the refrigerator tucked away in another corner of the room. Grabbing a bottle of cold water, I walked to the chair directly across from hers and took a seat.

"You should drink this water," I suggested, pushing the bottle atop the coffee table between us. Lauren looked at the bottle, but not at me, ultimately deciding she didn't want that either. "Drink the water."

Unlike the first statement, that wasn't a suggestion.

For the first time since entering the room, she met my eyes. Holding up her head with a bent arm along the couch's armrest, she glared at me. The anger in her eyes was almost overpowering.

"Don't tell... don't tell me what to... what to do."

"It'll make the room stop spinning," I offered.

"Oh, okay." She reached for the bottle, not needing more convincing than that. In spite of myself, I was endeared by this, holding back a smile.

I felt fortunate for having found Lauren when I did. Some people would run into a woman in her condition, and try to take advantage of how cooperative drunkenness makes people. With me, she was safe. I hoped she knew that.

"I'm sorry," Lauren apologized unexpectedly, passing a hand through her thick head of curls. Memories of me waking up in a bed with my face buried under all that hair flashed through my mind. If I focused a little harder, I could clearly remember the vanilla scent that once floated off of her. "For throwing up..." she hiccupped "...on you."

"It's just a shirt," I brushed it off.

"I'll pay you money," she whispered a promise. "Dry cleaning. For dry cleaning."

I raised my brows at the offer, hoping there was no way she thought I would take her money. "Don't worry about it."

She tiredly nodded, glancing at me quickly before looking back down at the water bottle she'd yet to open. Her eyes were lined with dark make up, a look on her I wasn't used to. On her body was a tight, strapless black dress, seemingly made with as little fabric as possible. My eyes traveled down the natural curves of her frame, something weight loss could never completely change. She was smaller, but that memorable shape of hers was still there.

Yeah, it was a good thing I found her when I did.

"How many shots did you take?"

Lauren rested her head on the couch's arm rest, drawing up her eyes to look at me when she replied, "Eight."

"*Goddamn.*" Six shots of *Hennessy* was enough to debilitate some grown men I knew. I could only imagine the havoc eight was wreaking on her. The state she was in was not going to die down any time soon.

"Is that...is that a lot?" she asked in response to my outburst. Lauren looked dizzy, her breathing a little shallow as she did everything she could to maintain a semblance of control. I didn't have to ask to know that she was slipping. She was getting to that zone where being drunk was no longer fun, but an ordeal. I moved from my seat across from her, taking the open seat at her side.

"Come on," I took her by the arm, taking the unopened water bottle from between her fingers and pulling her closer. Her hair pressed onto my chest, and just as I remembered, she smelled like vanilla, thrusting me into memories of holding her this close last summer. Uncapping the cool bottle, I wrapped an arm around her back, and brought the bottle to her lips. "Drink."

"I'm not...thirsty," she complained, pushing the bottle away weakly. If she had a problem with being in my arms right now, she didn't have the fight to protest it. "Not thirsty."

"Just drink half, then," I encouraged from behind her head.

"Don't force…" she hiccupped "…me."

I let out a sigh, trying not to get frustrated.

"Are you mad?" She turned her head to get a look at me. She was drunk, so she likely didn't even realize how close to my face she was, her lips literal inches from mine. I replied to her question with a shake of my head. In truth, I didn't know what I was feeling right now. From finding Lauren at the other end of that door to now, I hadn't exactly had time for reflection. I was operating on a form of instinct-driven autopilot.

Lauren wasn't okay, so—naturally—I had to take care of her.

It had been like this since the night we first met, and even after a sixteen-month stop in contact, this was still the case. There was no time to think about our history, or what any of this meant. I just knew she was here—and that she needed me.

"You're touching me," she seemed to finally notice, her eyes traveling along the arm I had wrapped around her. "Why are you touching…?"

"Lauren, I need you to—"

"I don't…belong to you," she interrupted, wanting to make sure I knew. The words rolled off my shoulders, not touching me in the way she intended them to. "I'm not… I'm not for everybody."

My brows came together, confused. "What?"

She shook her head, irritation crossing her expression at my not understanding, trying again to explain some other way. "I'm not dirty."

"Who said you were?"

"Everyone," she whispered after what felt like an hour-long silence. "With their eyes. The way they... the way that they look at me."

Her voice sounded so defeated.

Something in my chest twisted, understanding. "Lauren, you're not—"

She cut me off, pushing her hands against my shirt to create some distance. "I don't need you to..."

When she didn't finish her sentence, I set the bottle of water in my hand on the coffee table.

"Your fault," she mumbled, inching further away to the farthest corner of the couch we sat on, slipping out of my hold. "It's your fault that they... that they look at me like I'm dirty. Why they think they can touch me..."

"What do you mean?"

"You," she whined, her voice cracking. "You made me... like *this*."

"Like what?"

Her hand came up to catch the couple of tears that slipped out from her eyes.

"Tainted goods. Trash. Dirty. Whore. Slut... Worthless," she listed off the names like they were words imposed on her every day. And from the way that she cried, these likely were names she heard daily. In a way that only Lauren would ever know how to do, my heart broke.

It wasn't hard to understand.

I caught on with what she was trying to tell me immediately. Our relationship, as public as it was last summer, had left her branded in her world of bougie elitism.

Her involvement with me made her an outsider in the only world she'd ever known.

I moved to close the distance between us that she'd made, scooping her back up into my arms. She tensed up for a split second, and I waited for her to push me away. Instead, she let out a sigh, planting her face into the crook of my neck, her body shaking with silent sobs. I could feel her tears dropping hot against the bare skin of my neck, searing into me like acid.

"Did you come here by yourself?" I spoke quietly.

"I came with Rashad," she replied as if I would know who that was, the rise and fall of her speech hinting that she was still very intoxicated. "But I...but I want to go home."

"And he won't take you home?" I questioned.

"Paid too much...too much money to be here."

I had to check myself. With eyes closed, I drew in a calming inhale, willing my temper to not take hold right now. I was angry, but I had Lauren to look out for.

This nigga—Rashad, or whatever the fuck— brought Lauren, of all people, to a nightclub. He either let her drink eight shots of straight Hennessy, or left her by herself to drink alone. And now that her ass was drunk, asking to go home, he let her wander about the club until she ultimately—and luckily—showed up at my office door.

All on her *goddamn* birthday.

So many things could have happened to her.

I was livid, but I had Lauren to look out for.

With my free hand, I dug into my back pocket and pulled out my phone, bypassing the list of missed calls and probing texts messages I'd yet to respond to. After my meeting with Javier Perez, I was supposed to have gone downstairs into the VIP section with Eden because I told her I would, but when Lauren showed up at my door, those plans were put on the backburner. The half dozen texts from Eden on my phone were no doubt questioning my whereabouts.

Pulling up the dial pad, I quickly put in a number and pressed the phone to my ear.

Marlon answered on the second ring. The sound around him was quiet which let me know he'd skipped out on Eden's afterparty.

"What's up?"

"I need you to come to *Seven*," I got straight to it, explaining, "It's Lauren."

Pause. Silence. Realization. "Wait, *really*?"

He didn't sound like he believed me all the way.

"I'd take her home myself, but..." I thought about the things Lauren had revealed to me just a few moments ago. Her association with me wasn't helping anyone, especially her. "...it's complicated. Could you just do me this favor?"

"Uh..." My friend hesitated, something in his pause indicating he had more than just the one question he'd asked. Instead, Marlon let it go, ultimately conceding, "...yeah, I'll be there in a few."

"Who was that?" she asked against my neck as soon as the line went dead. Lauren's tone was croaky, like that of a woman's who just finished crying. There was a tinge of exhaustion in her voice as well.

"Do you remember Marlon?" I asked, my hand coming up behind her, rubbing soothing circles along the back of her dress. I could feel her nod, her head nuzzling into my neck. I wondered if the intimacy of the moment was due to her being drunk, or if this kind of stuff just came naturally for us. "He's gonna take you home."

The better part of my logic knew that this was only happening because she was drunk. After all, Lauren was a woman who believed I betrayed her in the worst possible way. As great as it felt to hold her in my arms, none of this was real, none of this would pan out if she was sober.

Is this right? Am I taking advantage right now?

"You feelin' better?" I checked to see if she was still crying. She didn't respond. Perhaps because the answer was clear. No. She wasn't feeling better. "You want my opinion?"

"No," she muttered against me, which actually made me laugh a little. Too drunk to act on the fact that she wanted nothing to do with me, but not drunk enough to forget to remind me that we weren't friends. To make sure there were no misunderstandings, she added, "I don't care... what you think."

I nodded, taking the blow in stride.

"That's fine, but you should keep that same energy with the people that got you so in your feelings right now," I suggested.

Lauren pulled away from me, her eyes drawing up to mine with cautious curiosity. I stared back, raising a hand to her tear-streaked cheeks, wiping away the moisture from them. She didn't cringe away from my touch, an observation that relieved something deep down within me. In that moment, it felt like we were closed off from our surroundings. Lauren's eyes searched for something in mine, her gaze analytical. I wondered if she could see anything in them, growing increasingly aware of how close her lips were to mine.

Cutting into the moment's silence, my phone began to vibrate.

Eye contact broke.

And the world around us seemed to come back.

"Can you stand?" I asked her, pulling up my cell to reply to Marlon's arrival text. He was downstairs and parked outside. Lauren hesitated a little before she replied, ultimately nodding an unconvincing yes. "That's alright. Hook your arms around my neck," I instructed, tucking an arm under her knees.

Arms around my neck clasped tight, her head pressed into my chest as I rose us both from the couch. Wanting to forgo the spectacle of walking through the main club, holding Lauren in my arms, I ambled over to an alternative exit from my second floor office. The second exit was a private stairwell that opened out to an alleyway between the club and another building.

Each step I took down that staircase felt like a reluctant goodbye. Lauren and I would part ways, she would eventually sober up, and life would go on.

Without her.

"Kain," she whispered my name during the descent, her voice gut wrenchingly soft. It was the first time I'd heard her say it in sixteen months. *Fuck, I even miss the way she used to say my name.* Lauren seemed to press the side of her face harder against my chest. "Kain, your heart's beating so fast."

"You're heavy," I lied.

I couldn't let her know that this uneventful ass half-hour was the highlight of my year so far. I wasn't the kind of nigga who was gonna tell my ex-girlfriend that I didn't want her to go because I missed her. I wouldn't even tell her that I missed her. I could be a lot of things for Lauren, but pathetic wasn't one of them.

The cool rush of December air nipped at her exposed skin as soon as we were outside. I could feel her shivering against me, and I felt regretful that I didn't have something with sleeves to give her.

Outside of the club, a crowd of photographers were huddled together, trying to keep warm as they waited for the afterparty to close out so they could get snapshots of the famous guests in attendance as they left.

As soon as I was spotted by one, they all began to crowd around like feeding ducks at a park. Their questions and camera flashes were nothing new, so it was easy for me to tune them out. Lauren brought her hands to her eyes, shielding them from the bright flashing.

Marlon's car was parked out front as he said it would be, and once Lauren and I were in view, noting my full hands, he stepped out of his car to open the back door. After the whole fiasco with the Eden dating rumors, I considered my requests of him now as a form of getting even.

"Cover me."

Marlon stood behind me as I buckled Lauren into the backseat of his car, making sure the gathering crowd of photographers wouldn't be able to get a good shot. Once Lauren was buckled in, I found myself lingering, looking over her as if I wanted to save a mental image of her for my memories.

She was so damn perfect. Had she always been this perfect? Did I appreciate it enough when she was mine? Her sleepy brown eyes watched me curiously, unblinking as her brows came together with an unspoken question. I couldn't read minds, but I knew what she was thinking. Because I was thinking the same thing: *So this is goodbye?*

Lauren didn't say anything when my hand came up to brush the stray curls at her forehead away. She didn't cringe under the unexpectedness of my touch. In fact, she leaned into it. Tucking the loose strands behind her ear, I pulled her in gently, pressing a kiss on to her forehead.

"Happy birthday, baby."

Chapter Ten

KAIN

"You smell like women's perfume," Eden mentioned when I took my seat beside her in *Seven's* VIP section.

"Yeah," I confirmed. "I probably do."

The media might've constantly hinted at the possibility of Eden and I being a couple, but that didn't make it true. We were friends—nothing more, nothing less. I wouldn't let magazines like *Fame Weekly* feed into some out-of-reach fantasy.

"You letting your hoes meet you outside your bedroom now? Looks like you got your shirts mixed up redressing yourself."

I pulled in close, whispering in Eden's ear, "Just so we're clear—you know you not my girlfriend, right?"

Her eyes shined with an unspoken laugh, playful and lively. She was giggling when she replied, "Dude, I know. It's just that all of America thinks I am, and I can't have you embarrassing me in these streets."

"Your first concert was a great success, Eden. You don't need rumors to sell tickets no more."

"A *great* success," she repeated, leaning in to grab a champagne flute on the table in front of us. "I must be in the twilight zone because that actually sounded like a compliment."

"Take it as one," I offered with a slight smile.

"You're in a better mood than usual," she noted, placing a hand on my forehead to jokingly check if I was burning up. Around us, the few people who were allowed in the VIP area watched us like they were getting an inside look on a romance that didn't actually exist. "I guess whoever Ms. *La Vie Est Belle* is, she's got the juice."

My smile faded.

"Uh-oh," Eden noticed immediately. "Was it something I said?"

I shook my head, ready to move onto something else. "Can I ask you something?"

"Go ahead, Kain."

"Do you still think about your exes when you get drunk?"

Eden chuckled at first, crossing her arms. "Who says I think about my exes ever?"

"Your debut album is titled *EX*."

"Those are also my initials, boy." She swatted at my shoulder, eventually getting to the truth when her smile disappeared. "But yeah... I wrote that entire album about this guy I dated when I was at Berklee." With a shake of her head she muttered, "*Fuck* that guy."

I wasn't curious about the relationship as much as I was curious about the effect it had on her.

"You can't imagine yourself downing eight shots of *Hennessy* one night and just finding yourself crying on his shoulder?"

"First of all," Eden started, setting her champagne flute back down, "I don't know what kind of death wish I'd have to have to take eight shots of *Hennessy* in one—"

"Focus," I redirected her back to the point.

"To answer your question, no. If I get drunk, I'm not calling his ass. I'm not texting his ass. I'm not missing his ass. I'm not even thinking about his ass."

"Because...?"

"*Becauuuuuuse*," she stretched out the word, looking at me from the tops of her eyes. "Because the feelings aren't there. *Obviously*. Why do you ask? You still thinking about your summer thing from last year?"

Eden passed a hand through her brown and green hair, twisting a strand around her finger, and waited for my response. I didn't say anything at first, choosing to take a moment to think about what tonight meant. I knew not to get ahead of myself. I knew it wouldn't be wise to expect a knock on my door in the morning, with Lauren waiting on the other side, telling me that something about how this current reality felt wrong, and asking for clarity.

I guess it could be said that part of me hoped that day both did and didn't come. If Lauren ever sought me out looking for answers, I would either have to reinforce the lie, or tell her the truth. Neither of those options were high on my bucket list.

Dr. Eloise said what I was doing all this time could be seen as a form of self-harm.

Personally, I considered it sacrifice. I was choosing someone else over myself.

"Is that why you were late?" Eden asked, cutting into the lull in our conversation. "Your boo thing from last summer put away eight shots of *Henny* and cried on your shoulder?" Eden flicked her eyebrows upward briefly, murmuring to herself, "Messy…"

* * *

In Miami's entertainment district, the last call time doesn't exist.

If they so please, nightclubs can remain open twenty-four hours a day. Of course, the cost benefit analysis of keeping a club open for that long was poor, so the latest that most Montgomery clubs would stay open was five o'clock in the morning.

At *Seven*, however, we stayed open—you guessed it—two extra hours.

The club was a complete ghost town by the time the clock struck five. I was sitting at the bar, stirring the ice in my glass of water. The only other person who was here was the bartender. His name was Joshua or Jose—something with a J—and he wiped down the bar counter in silence as I watched the ice in my glass melt.

Four hours before, I'd gotten an all-clear text from Marlon, confirming that Lauren had been safely dropped off. However, not at her parents' house, he revealed. Lauren had requested to be taken to her best friend's apartment in the Miami Park West neighborhood.

"Were you working the bar the whole night?" I asked the only other person in the room.

He stood up straight at the sound of my question—revealing his silver nametag pinned to the right strap of his black apron. Ahh, I was close—the guy's name was Josiah.

"I was."

"Just you?"

He nodded at the question, not really seeing what I was trying to discern by asking. That is, until I concluded, "So you're the nigga that thought it would be a good idea to let a lightweight drink half a bottle of Hennessy in one go."

Quickly, he got to making excuses, his hands coming up opened, as if getting ready for me to throw blows. "Yo, I knew that that was a bad idea."

"But you did it anyway."

"You don't understand—she had this pout, and these big brown eyes that just—"

He stopped talking in response to what could have only been the look on my face. I was not sitting around with this nigga, trying to have a conversation about how compelling Lauren's beauty was.

I'd been in his shoes once—pouring Lauren drinks she couldn't handle because she looked at me a certain way. I knew exactly what he meant when he talked about her eyes. But when I'd given in to them last year, she nearly got herself raped. And tonight could have been just as catastrophic if she hadn't stumbled upon my office.

Just before I could say anything else, Josiah reached under the bar's counter and placed a purse on the surface.

"It's not hard to guess that you're about to fire me," he stated, pulling the tie in his apron loose. "I apologize for my judgement, and I hope my being fired is the worst of it."

What a long winded way of requesting that a person refrain from knocking your teeth in.

A lot of things could have happened to Lauren due to Josiah's oversight, but the worst of it was the fact she'd thrown up on my shirt, and a guaranteed hangover come sunrise. Nothing truly bad had actually occurred, so for this, I didn't feel the need to get my hands dirty. Firing him would be just fine.

"What's with the bag?" was all I said in response.

"She left it here. And since you seem like you know her..." I suppose the anger in my eyes made that fact clear. "...I guess I'll leave it with you and get going."

I reached for the purse as Josiah tucked his folded apron under the counter. He left in a hurry, seemingly thankful that the loss of his job was the worst of it, and wanting to leave the building in case I changed my mind. When the main door closed behind him, I was truly alone in the disheveled party aftermath.

Out of curiosity, with the purse in my hand, I checked for what was inside.

"Of course," I said to myself, pulling out undisputable necessities from the pockets of her bag. A phone, a wallet, house and car keys—practically her whole life. If I were a spiritual person, I would've taken this as a sign.

* * *

Lauren

I woke up in a cloud.

Around me, a bleached white duvet covered my body, keeping me warm in a bed of plush softness. Even though I knew I wasn't in my room, I didn't immediately go into a panic.

No, this place was familiar.

I sat up, holding my head in my hands so I could get a better look of my surroundings. The sunlight hit my eyes then, and in that moment, it was like setting a fire alarm off in my head. I rushed to shield my eyes, scanning the room around me until I realized where I was.

"Lux!" I called out into the emptiness of the bedroom. This was her apartment, so I knew she had to be close by. "Ouch."

Shouting out loud did something to aggravate a dull headache I only realized I had after I spoke.

Great, I'm hungover.

What happened last night?

Between the sheets of Lux's bed, I only wore a borrowed night gown that I didn't remember changing into the night before. I wracked my brain, images flashing in my mind and coming in clusters, broken and discontinuous. Which parts were memories and which parts were dreamed? *Did I really see Kain last night?*

I patted the bedding around me, hoping to find my phone somewhere close by, only to come into contact with just plush, white sheets. Nothing. Rising to my feet, I went for the blinds first, eager to block out the room's sunlight because the brightness of it all was only worsening my headache.

"Lux," I called out more quietly as I walked the halls of her quaint one-bedroom apartment in the city. It wasn't until I reached the main area that I found my friend sitting at her kitchen island, headphones in on loud, looking like she'd just come in from the gym. I pulled one of her headphones out. "Girl, what happened last night?"

Lux's eyebrows came together confusedly before she broke into a smile.

"Shit, you say that like I was invited, birthday girl," she replied, pulling out the other earbud. My friend hopped off the kitchen stool, patting my cheek like a proud parent. "I don't know what happened. All I know is that you showed up at my door at almost two o'clock in the morning, ugly drunk, being carried bridal-style by a dude who definitely wasn't Rashad."

"Huh?" I pulled at her arm, leading her to a couch in her living room. "A dude? Who? Was it Kain?"

"Girl, what?" Lux squinted a grimace, shaking her head and creeping closer to me on the couch. "No. He was fine as hell, though. He didn't look like he'd come from the club, however. You were dressed like a lil' hoe in your black dress, looking sexy as hell. But he showed up in a hoodie and sweats, carrying you like y'all just got hitched."

I could only look at her with uncertainty. Lux's descriptions were doing nothing to jog my memory. In fact, she was only confusing me more.

"Are you cheating on Rashad? 'Cause if your side dudes look like *that*, I'm here for it, babe."

"I don't know." I shrugged. "I don't know if I cheated. Did the dude give you a name?"

"Xavier," Lux replied.

"Xavier?"

With a nod, my friend explained him even more, "He was about... this tall, and I swear to God he looked just like a light skinned Alfred Enoch."

"Xavier?" I questioned again. The name didn't ring a bell. At least, not as a first name. "Marlon maybe?"

"Yes!" Lux replied excitedly like we were playing a trivia game. "Yes, that was it! Marlon Xavier. Okay, so obviously y'all talked. So what's the tea?"

"We didn't talk," I sighed, leaning my head backwards against the back cushion of the couch. My hangover and the excited loudness of Lux's voice were not a good mix. "Marlon is a friend of Kain's."

The images in my mind weren't from dreams.

I really did see Kain last night. Another fresh memory came to me, causing me to cringe.

"I think I threw up on him last night."

"On who? Sweatpants Bae?"

"No!" I answered, knowing it would hurt to laugh at how silly she was. "On Kain."

"Ohhh," she replied, catching what I said last minute. "Wait—on *Kain*? When did you see Kain?"

"Last night, I think."

"Well where was Rashad in all of this?"

I shook my head, pulling a blank for the answer to that question. "I don't remember."

"You should call him. Maybe he knows what happened."

"Did Marlon have my purse when he brought me up?" I asked. "My phone was in my purse. Where is it?"

"The only thing he came up with was you," Lux revealed, adding for good measure, "With his *fine* ass…"

"Ahh, fuck," I muttered, taking my hungover little head into my hands. "I think I left my purse at *Seven* last night. Could you call my phone for me? Maybe whoever has it will pick up and agree to meet us."

"Wishful thinking for Miami," Lux mumbled, pulling up her cellphone and pressing in my speed dial number. The phone rang four times before going to voicemail. It would go to voicemail three more times before Lux decided to give up and send a text that read: **Phone lost. Call # 7865550001**.

The message was short enough to show up completely on the phone's lock screen, and for now, I could only hope that the person who found my stuff didn't want to keep it.

* * *

Both of my parents' cars were parked in the driveway when Lux pulled up to the front of my house. It was a little after five o'clock in the afternoon, with most of my day spent with my best friend, our time together closing off with a late birthday lunch at the mall.

"I'd stop in, but I figure since I'm in the neighborhood, I should at least visit my parents," Lux explained, as if she didn't come down from her newly leased apartment once a week to visit her parents. All my life, my best friend had always lived directly across the street from me. When she got her own apartment last spring, it was like a blessing for me as well—the perfect getaway option.

But getaways couldn't last forever.

My mother was in the kitchen, quietly preparing dinner when I walked in. For as long as I could remember, my home had always been quiet. Sometimes the diplomatic levels of noiselessness came off as sterile, as cold. It made it feel like there was no love here, even though I'd spent years telling myself there was.

When she heard my footsteps pitter pat behind her in the silence, she immediately turned. I expected a, *'Happy birthday, Lori,'* but what I got was a, "Your father wants to see you in his office."

"Why?" I asked her cautiously, anxiety already firing up from within me. My hangover had died down some, but not nearly enough to handle it if Daddy had something to shout at me for. "Am I in trouble?"

Mom looked at me, her face like mine and Morgan's, save for a few differences here and there, and the addition of time. "If you have to ask...?" She raised an eyebrow. "Go on, Lori. The longer you stall, the more time he has to sit on it."

"Sit on what?"

"Go."

My feet dragged against the mahogany floors spread throughout my house. Goosebumps rose along my skin in anticipation for what this unexpected chat with my father might be. If Dr. Eloise could catch a glimpse of the anxiety levels in my body, she would quickly make sure I knew that the relationship I had with my father couldn't have possibly been a healthy one.

But that was us, though. Dysfunctional. Especially as of late—like two ill fitting parts being forced together to create some semblance of togetherness. I longed for the days I could move out of my parents' house the way my best friend had already done. Only then would I be spared from the hair graying stress of being *'called into my father's office'*.

I knocked twice before entering, noting the slight shake of my hand as I did it.

A girl should not be this afraid of her father. This is not natural.

When I stepped into my father's private space, I found his office overrun with a heap of campaign swag. *Caplan For Governor 2018* on just about everything you could think of from t-shirts to lawn signs, a campaign headquarters nestled away into the far back corners of my childhood home.

"Hey, Daddy," I greeted him quietly, cautiously stepping into crowded space.

He didn't say anything at first, but I could just tell from the look on his face that this wasn't some elaborate way of pranking me into a birthday surprise. No. My father was angry. About what, I didn't know, but somehow I knew it tied into the previous night I was having trouble remembering.

"Lauren," he started, voice somber, like a person who'd done everything he could to salvage something, and still couldn't succeed. "You know, I really loved my job. From the moment I knew what a state's attorney was, I put my everything into becoming one. Sleepless nights. Day in, day out. I was dedicated." He pulled out a folder from the top of a stack of papers on his desk. "Last year, I lost that job. Lost that dream."

"I'm sorry Daddy." I've apologized for this over a hundred times.

"And for a very long time, I felt like my life as I knew it was over. But then this opportunity to run for office came along. I've run a good campaign; my poll numbers are high. No negative press," He paused, looking at me with eyes so venomous you'd think that he hated me. "Until now."

Slowly he opened the folder in front of him, pulling out a single sheet of color printed paper—a photograph. I reached for the sheet, my stomach heavy with stress, and dropping when I was finally able to make out what I was seeing.

A picture of me.

Wearing the dress I had on the night before, I was nestled comfortably within Kain Montgomery's arms, my arms clinging around his neck as he carried me out in the open. The picture didn't give away much, but two things were abundantly clear—one, I needed to be carried out of a nightclub, which came with obvious insinuations, and two, it appeared as if I was still associated with Kain Montgomery.

I cringed.

My father pulled out several more photos—my face covered in most of them, although Kain's was not. There were dozens, however, and any one of them could make the front page given the right headline.

Candidate Caplan's Daughter Still Seeing Kain Montgomery.

Lauren Caplan & Kain Montgomery: The Saga Continues.

Is Kain Montgomery CHEATING On Eden Xavier?! How A Summer Fling Became The Sidepiece.

The last photo my father pulled out was the most damning. Kain crouching low beside a car's open back seat, a single hand holding my face, pressing a kiss onto my forehead. Objectively speaking, with no context, the photo could have been seen as sweet. I couldn't remember the kiss, but from the photo alone, it looked tender... warm... *loving*.

I shook away that last thought.

Kain Montgomery never loved you. At least, not for real. It was all a scam.

My inner thoughts talked me out of the heart flutter I felt coming on. I only saw love in that photo because that's what some unconscious part of me wanted to see.

"The photographer who took these photos is shopping them around to all the major news outlets," my father explained. "Montgomery is allegedly in a high profile relationship with some popstar, so these photos are a double whammy—celebrity cheating scandal *and* political ammunition. Do you know what the papers will say about me when these photos go public? My campaign—all of it—in the garbage. Who can expect me to run a state when I can't even run my own daughter?!"

I shrunk under the volume of his words, wanting to cry, but not allowing myself to. "Is it possible to just buy the pictures?" I asked quietly.

"Do you have eighty grand lying around somewhere that I don't know about? Of course we tried to buy them, but coupled with the celebrity cheating scandal potential the photos have, they're charging just under a hundred thousand for them. Lauren, it's over. I hope you realize what you've done!"

"What about the campaign funds?"

Millions of dollars had been donated to my fathers campaign. I couldn't see why he didn't just—

Dad's fist slammed into the wood of his desk, sounding off like indoor thunder. "Spend donor money for this? My constituents would eat me alive if word ever got out that I used their money so that my *whore* of a daughter could sneak around with thugs in the dead of night unchecked!"

My lower lip began to tremble, and I had to bite into it to keep myself composed. He was so angry. So... hateful. Sometimes I couldn't be sure that my father didn't absolutely despise me. It just felt like I was always doing something to make him unhappy.

Last year, after he'd kicked me out, Morgan would go on to tell me that, that summer Dad wouldn't even stay in the same room as a person who wanted to talk about me. Mom wanted me home, but Dad was content to never see me again. That is, until I got shot. Morgan would go on to tell me that my shooting made Dad soften up a little. She said it was clear he felt guilty about it, like he was taking partial responsibility for what had happened.

I lied awake at night wondering if my father let me come home because he loved me, or if it was because he felt sorry for me. Mom tried to be a little more forthcoming, her behavior towards me the same as it had always been. She didn't treat me any differently for what I'd done. However, she didn't stand up for me either. It never used to cross my mind when I was a Daddy's Girl, but this past year had really showed me that my mother walked on eggshells with my father.

When it came to my mother, I realized that she would never do anything that would start a fight. It was a realization that made me feel powerless, like no one in the world was in my corner. She let my father kick me out of a house they shared, and in order to keep him content, she didn't even look for me. I used to think my parents had a good marriage. When I finally opened my eyes, I realized that this was not the case. My parents didn't have a good marriage; my father merely had a very submissive wife.

And he wanted to mold his daughters into that submission as well.

"Daddy, I'm so sorry." I sounded like I was pleading. And maybe I was pleading—apologizing as if to say, *Daddy please don't hate me*.

"Rashad's been calling the house all day, and been saying you won't pick up his calls." My father shook his head, his eyes cutting into me as if I were disgusting. "So that's what you do? You mess around on a good young man for the love of some criminal. Did you sleep with him last night? Is that where you've been all day—in his bed?"

"Daddy, I lost my ph—"

"It's a simple yes or no question, Lauren. I don't wanna hear any more apologies and excuses. If you can play like you grown, then be grown. Quit your whining, and answer my question. Did you... *fuck*... that thug... last night?"

"I didn't." There was nothing I could do to stop the single tear that ran down my cheek. Instead, I rushed to wipe it away, all too eager to act like it never existed. "I really didn't. I was with Lux last night. I didn't do anything."

"You liar!" More fist punching into his desk, cracking like manmade thunder. Every time he hit his desk, I wondered if some small part of him wished it was me he was hitting. "It wasn't enough that you humiliated me last year, running around with that degenerate, getting yourself knocked up with his spawn. You don't know how to control yourself. You must like the fact that any self-respecting person within a fifty mile radius sees you as a run-through whore. You're trying to drag this family's name down to your level."

I crumbled, my hands going to my ears, blocking out even the sounds of my cries begging him to stop. I could hear myself apologizing over and over and over, my voice growing more unstable with each apology I uttered. Even though, I'd done nothing wrong, I felt guilty. I had to fix this. "What... wh-what do you... w-want me to... do?"

If my father told me I would make his life easier by drowning in the ocean, in that moment, I would've started making my way to the beach. I hadn't really done anything the night before, but the vitriolic hatred in his rant made me apologize for things I knew I didn't do. Anything to make him stop yelling at me.

"I just want you to stop, Lauren," Dad replied, his volume finally coming down, yet completely unfazed by the fact that I was falling to pieces before his eyes. "Stop disappointing me."

Chapter Eleven

KAIN

No one slept in my bed last night.

Well, no one aside from me. This was the first time that happened in three months. Over the last hundred days, a permanent fixture in my bed had been, as Eden would call it, "one of my hoes." Dr. Eloise once said I was on a predictable spiral that only arose when a person was trying to fill a void. And so every night, for three months, I tried to fill it. Last night, however, I broke the streak.

Coupled with the fact that I'd arrived at my apartment at six o'clock that morning, I simply wasn't in the mood to entertain guests at the moment.

I hadn't always been like this.

After Lauren woke up last summer, I waited for her. With all that waiting, it took me a very long time to get to this point. For twelve straight months, I remained faithful to a woman who wasn't even mine anymore.

It was a weird pact of celibacy that I deluded myself into believing would bring her back. I refused to get anyone else for fear it would only make the separation more legitimate. So I waited, getting to some of my lowest points to date. I was always of the belief that the worst thing someone I cared about could do was die.

It was Lauren that taught me that this wasn't the case.

The worst thing someone I cared about could do to me was act as if I was dead to them.

Six months ago, I'd finally moved out of Silas' house. I was the last person to leave. With Silas in jail and my uncle living in the old safe house in Pembroke Pines, the already gigantic house on the beach seemed to only get bigger. The place was filled with memories—some bad, some good—though, it was my own bedroom that I couldn't stand to be in anymore.

The sheets on my bed could have been washed a thousand times, switched out, or even thrown away. I swore her ghost still slept within them. Lauren's continued absence didn't stop me from waking up some nights, feeling if she was there, hoping that everything leading up to now had just been a really vivid nightmare.

I missed her.

I missed her in ways that made me feel like I was being subjected to cruel and unusual punishment. I didn't know you could long for someone so strongly that it resonates to your bones. It was like feeling empty was a part of my identity now.

And I withstood it all because the alternative was to take everything I was feeling, and put it on her. Trade in my pain for hers? I couldn't do it. She'd been through so much already.

However, I learned last night, that even as I did all that I could to protect her, Lauren was still suffering. That much was clear from the way she cried on my shoulder the night before. It wasn't until she brought it to my attention that it dawned on me that there were some things I'd just never be able to protect her from.

But that didn't mean I didn't try.

Last year, when I decided I wasn't going to tell Lauren about the lengths her father would go, I did so with the belief that when it came to Lauren's wellbeing, her father was the only one I needed to look out for. Joshua Caplan had shot his daughter, and then leveraged her life in order to get me to stand as a witness for my father's trial. Shooting Lauren may have been an accident, but that didn't mean I was going to take a step back and assume Lauren was safe with him.

A few days after I'd received Lauren's restraining order last year, I found myself at in a meeting the least likely of candidates.

Joshua Caplan, himself.

* * *

August 24th, 2016
(Sixteen Months Ago)

Caplan looked haggard. It was days after the scene at the court, and it was my guess that the media attention that came with the spectacle was starting to weigh heavily on him.

The man looked stressed.

"I know you shot her," I got straight to the point once he sat down. I didn't come here to make small talk. Caplan was a seasoned attorney. It was his job to know how to lie, and do it well. So when I levied my accusation, of course he got to pleading his own case, getting the outrage in his voice just perfect. "Save your energy. I know you were aiming for me."

We were tucked away in the booth of some isolated diner just off I-95, nestled deep within Overtown. Overtown was one of the rougher parts of Miami, but I liked this community, and this community liked me. My family had a lot of influence over the residents here. As property developers made their way in, the look of the neighborhood was starting to change. It seemed like there was a new high-end apartment building being built here every day.

The real Overtown community was getting priced out of the homes they'd lived in all their lives, and it was my family that kept a lot of these people from being on the streets. For that, I was always welcomed here. Which was why I liked the little diner off I-95. It was a good place to have meetings like this. There were never too many people here, and it was always open.

It was a late night, and as Caplan realized I figured out what he'd done, he looked over his shoulder as if he expected assassins to pop out from the shadows at any moment. He thought this was a set up.

Nah...

I couldn't kill Lauren's father no matter how much I wanted to. She loved this monster. I'd spent an entire summer watching Lauren's spirit dull with every day her parents made no effort to get into contact with her. It was true that the summer we'd spent together was beautiful, filled with love at every turn, but Lauren was not the kind of girl who could just up and forget that she had a family.

The sadness in her eyes, which she often tried to hide from me, was a testament to that fact.

"What's all this for?" Caplan questioned, his head still whipping around suspiciously. He had to have known I had something on him. Why else would he have gotten in his car and driven several miles out to meet me here?

I had thought about what I was going to say at least two dozen times on the drive up. I thought about the threats I would make. I wondered if I was going to be able to look this man in his face and keep my hands to myself. I saw this moment playing out in my head a million different ways, and none of them started out with me asking, "Is she okay?"

But it was the first thing I asked.

He squinted, unsure if this was my way of trying for some elaborate joke. *'This is what he made me meet him for?'* his eyes seemed to question.

"Is she okay?" I repeated the question, not realizing until I asked it a second time that I desperately needed to know. Caplan may have shot her, but that didn't stop me from feeling like I shared in some of the blame. It supposed to have been me. I moved out of the way. And so it was her.

The memory of her body weakening in my arms sent a shiver down my spine and lit a match in my mind. I was looking at the person who did it to her, wanting nothing more than to reach across the table, take his neck within the palm of my hand, and squeeze.

But I wouldn't.

I couldn't.

"She's getting stronger," he said finally, and I noted the air of remorse in his response. "What's all this for?"

"Would you have really pulled the plug on her if I hadn't agreed to testify?"

Guilt flashed across his features, and I knew his answer before he said it. Yeah... He would've pulled the plug. "We didn't actually think she'd wake up," he confessed.

I guess I'd bought Lauren just the right amount of time she needed. I took it that Caplan's 'we' meant that even Lauren's mother also would've been on board with cutting off her life support. The realization made me feel an odd mixture of anger and... relief. I could lose my mind over life's what-ifs—what if she'd taken a little longer to wake—but thankfully, I didn't have to.

She was here.

Alive.

That's all that mattered.

"You know the only thing keeping me from reachin' across that table is her, right?"

"And the witnesses," Caplan reminded, motioning toward the diner staff and the one or two other people having late-night meals inside. He thought that meant something to me.

Nah, this was Miami.

Contrary to whatever power he felt like law enforcement had here, I *owned* this city.

Especially now that Silas was locked away somewhere for a crime he didn't commit.

"Fuck the witnesses." I leaned across the table, eyes unblinking as I glared at the older, fair-skinned man across from me. "You're only alive 'cause she needs you."

Lauren would sooner heal from the pain of my alleged betrayal, than the pain of her father's betrayal. I wasn't delusional enough to fool myself into thinking I could ever compete with the love women had for their dads. Having four sisters taught me a lot about that kind of bond. In these trying times, more than anything—more than friends, more than doctors, more than me... More than anything, Lauren needed her family.

"And so what am I here for?" Caplan asked.

"'Cause I understand people like you," I replied quietly. "I understand what's about to happen. You are gonna look at that girl everyday and see her as somebody who ruined *your* life, not the other way around. That's what selfish people are like. She's your fuckin' daughter, but I already know you're not gonna to think about her, about what she needs to heal, about how she sleeps at night, if she's eating enough, if she's happy."

"You've got a lot of nerve to—"

"Don't finish that statement," I cut in. "It's wildly ironic. You shot her, remember? *I've* got a lot of nerve? Nah, you dumbass... I just *love* her." Something he clearly couldn't wrap his head around because narcissists don't understand what it means to love someone. Lauren's father sat back, his look of skepticism holding firm until he'd stared me down long enough to realize I wasn't bullshitting. What was skepticism in his eyes before turned into caution, unsureness in what was coming next. I released a sigh. "And so here's what you're gonna do..."

* * *

December 16th, 2017
(Present Day)

Every week, I got a bill from Dr. Eloise's office for two weekly therapy sessions.

However, I only saw Dr. Eloise once a week. Every Monday at noon.

The other session was for Lauren. Mondays at four. About a year and a half ago, after a hostile conversation with Joshua Caplan at a shabby Overtown diner, I took on the cost to ensure that Lauren, even in my absence, was not being neglected.

In trying to understand Joshua Caplan, I would always ask myself, '*What would Silas do?*' and then I'd have my answer. Would Silas, having as much money as he did, ever think to send any one of my sisters to a professional if that's what they needed?

Absolutely not.

So, naturally, it was safe to assume Caplan would be the same way. They were more alike than they were different—my father and Lauren's. It helped a lot in terms of making me aware of who I was dealing with.

Despite the fact that I always knew where Lauren would be at four o'clock every Monday, I never waited around in the parking lot, or anything, to get a glimpse of her. I was always out of the building and home long before Lauren would even get there.

Paying for the therapy wasn't a control thing for me.

I paid for it because I knew she wouldn't have anyone to talk to about all of this. I knew Lauren better than most, if not better than everyone, and I knew no one in her world of upper middle class exceptionalism was ever going to understand what she'd been through. Not even her best friend.

Footing the bill for the appointments didn't grant me some special insight into what went on in Lauren's sessions either. No matter who paid for the appointments, Dr. Eloise adhered by a strict set of laws that forbade her from even mentioning that she knew Lauren.

But of course Dr. Eloise was aware that I knew Lauren was one of her clients.

The bills were in my name after all.

Always the professional, though, Dr. Eloise didn't say anything about it to me. We carried on in our sessions as if Lauren wouldn't be sitting in the same exact seat three hours after I left. I didn't even ask. I simply relied on the faith that whatever was happening in Dr. Eloise's sessions with Lauren, was helping her heal.

Seeing Lauren's emotional state from last night made me lose a little confidence in the effectiveness of her therapy, though. Lauren went to just as many appointments as I did, and while I felt the sessions with Dr. Eloise served me well, the Lauren I saw last night seemed more broken than I could've ever imagined.

Maybe it was naïve of me to think that just because she needed her parents, it would mean they would actually be there for her. The girl that I saw last night was very clearly deteriorating slowly.

It was something that haunted me throughout the entire day, making me wonder if I needed to rethink my approach. Did she need me? Or did I just really want to believe she did?

I was sitting in the living room of my apartment when a call came through on my cell phone. It was Eden's manager, likely calling to confirm the purchase of photos I'd put in early this morning before I went to bed.

"Did you get all of them?" was the greeting I chose to answer the phone call with. Eden's manager was a no-nonsense older woman who was very good at her job, so I wasn't surprised when she made a sound of confirmation. "I appreciate it, Lily."

The photos I'd bought, using Eden's manager as my middleperson, went to market at six-thirty this morning, being shopped to gossip magazines and large scale blogs. That's why I stayed up so late; I wanted to be awake to make the first bid. The pictures of me carrying Lauren to Marlon's car the night before were never going public now. Lily might've thought I was buying the pictures to avoid being accused of cheating on Eden, but that wasn't the case at all. After all, Eden and I were friends at best.

It also wasn't like me to buy paparazzi shots in order to keep stories from going public. I never cared that much. The pictures I bought, that was for Lauren's sake.

Setting my phone down on the coffee table in front of me, I picked up another. I'd fallen asleep this morning around eight, and when I woke up at around noon, the rose gold iPhone Lauren had left at *Seven* the night before (along with the rest of her stuff) was lighting up once every five minutes with text messages. It had been ringing off the hook before I'd fallen asleep as well.

I tried to mind my own business.

Lauren's text messages weren't for me to snoop through. Most of the messages she'd received today were, from what I could see from her lock screen, birthday wishes. However, it was one name that kept popping up, seemingly desperate to get a hold of her.

He had already called her thirty-eight times and it wasn't even six o'clock yet.

Lauren had said his name the night before, identifying him as the man she'd shown up at *Seven* with.

The one who wouldn't take her home because entry to the party had been too expensive. It would be a lie if I said I didn't have questions, if there wasn't some part of me that wanted to know who she'd replaced me with.

I'd been telling myself that for me to even try to guess her passcode and snoop around in her personal life would be some bitch made behavior. But the curiosity was mounting, every time another one of his text messages or calls went through, I found my finger lingering on the keypad, talking myself out of trying to get in.

When Lauren was mine, I knew that the passcode to her phone was her birthday, December 16th, 1996. It was so easy, I could just press it in and...

1-2-1-6-9-6

The phone in my hand vibrated with an error, meaning that was no longer her passcode. That should've been my cue to set the phone down and quit while I was ahead, but now it wasn't so much as a desire to see what was in the phone, but a desire to see if I still knew her well enough to guess.

6-9-6-1-2-1

Her birthday backwards wasn't the code either.

I went on to try six different possibilities, from her address to even my own birthday; all wrong. Just as I was beginning to think the code must've tied into something new about her that I didn't know, an idea crossed my mind. A leap was what it was, but it was the last six-number code that I could think to try. I keyed in the numbers expecting yet another error vibration.

0-3-0-4-1-6

The error message never came. With the input of the last number, Lauren's phone unlocked, and my chest tightened with the revelation. No, her passcode wasn't her birthday. It wasn't my birthday. It wasn't her address. It wasn't her name numerically. None of that.

Lauren's passcode, after all this time, was the day that we first met.

Chapter Twelve

Lauren

I skipped dinner.

Mom and Dad were inside, alright with having a quiet meal without me. Morgan was, of course, out with friends as today was her birthday as well. I sat on a white porch swing, swinging back and forth under the glow of nearby streetlights.

Today was a bad day.

Sitting out on the front porch, I wished that Monday would come sooner. I could tell Dr. Eloise about these past couple of days—Rashad at the club, my father just a couple hours earlier. It was hard to not feel like I must've done something terrible to have earned the position I found myself in as of late.

Being alone is a sad feeling.

Even worse, being alone when you're surrounded by others—that was the type of thing to truly break a person down. It used to be that I would have days like this, and immediately call my friend Lux. These days, I no longer felt as comfortable opening up to her. She barely noticed the changes in my willingness to be open with her, but I certainly did. I was far more reserved with her than I'd previously been.

When I was in the hospital last year, Lux took it upon herself to speak to the press about my relationship with Kain, painting him as some sort of predator. I understood why she would do such a thing; she was only trying to look out for me and make sure the people who had harmed me were punished. However, the interviews Lux gave painted me as some naïve child. To hear the way she spoke about me to the media, it became clear that she saw me as some fickle-minded girl who fell prey to the treacherous ways of the malicious Kain Montgomery.

I didn't know she felt that way about me.

Maybe I was asking for a lot, but I would've thought it reasonable to expect my friends to not have such a low opinion of my judgement. Lux had called me stupid for trusting Kain many times, but it wasn't until I woke up last year and saw the interviews that she'd given, that I realized she meant it wholeheartedly.

My best friend thought I was stupid for falling for Kain Montgomery.

It wasn't an unforgivable thought for her to have had. Hell, I felt stupid for falling for Kain Montgomery. I still felt stupid for the small parts of me that refused to let him go even now. It's just that... if the roles had been reversed, I would not have gotten on a public platform and reinforced some idea that Lux was dumb and childish—even if I did feel that way. I wouldn't have added to the public humiliation ritual the media was so hellbent on putting me through.

Lux meant well, so of course I didn't hate her for the part she'd played in the media circus, but the damage was done.

I didn't trust her like I used to.

So I sat alone, swinging back and forth in the dimming twilight of the early evening, staring outward unto the purpling Miami sky. Inside the house behind me, my parents were likely finishing up dinner. I think some part of them were relieved that I didn't want to eat with them. Whenever I had dinner with my parents, and Morgan was not around, dinner droned on painfully slow. It was always awkward. My parents didn't know how to interact with me anymore.

The quiet and empty street touching the frontside of my home was soothing. I had privacy. Here, I could wipe away at my tears, away from the prying eyes of my household, but get the much needed space to breathe that my bedroom couldn't provide. Plus, the Christmas lights that twinkled outside gave me a comforting brush of nostalgia. I'd always loved Christmas. It reminded me of a simpler time.

Sometimes I thought about dropping out of my classes, getting a part-time job somewhere, and trying to start over on my own. These thoughts usually got loudest on my worst days. When things would get especially bad, I would delve into an exceedingly avoided habit, and think about Kain. Logic would remind me that he never loved me, but that didn't stop me from craving the security of his arms when my emotions got to be this bad.

When I was sad last summer, Kain used to have this way of wrapping his arms around my shoulders from behind, holding my back to his chest while the tip of his chin rested on the back of my head. '*Just breathe, baby*,' he used to whisper into my hair. '*I've got you.*'

I hated myself for missing it all so much—the security of his embrace, the fresh scent of his skin, the way I could feel the sound waves of his voice vibrate along my back when he spoke. I missed the little things, too, like the way he said my name, like even just the word was worthy of being treated with care. Even though it was all fake, I missed it.

I sniffled once, hearing the sound of footsteps cutting into the silence around me. I turned my head, half expecting one of my parents to be walking up from behind, but they were nowhere to be seen. Whipping my head around, I searched for the source of the sound. When my eyes landed on the athletic figure standing at the end of my parents' driveway, I stopped breathing.

This isn't happening.

He stood there, comfortably standing still when we locked eyes under the dim light of the setting sky. In his hands, he held a medium-sized bag, the kind of bag that usually held gifts. I wondered if he got me something for my birthday, only to shake away the thought because even if he did, I didn't want it.

"Hey."

It was a single word, uttered out of the mouth of a man I'd been thinking about only seconds before. Less than a minute ago, I swore that I longed for this man. And now that he was here, standing at the end of my driveway as if I'd magically manifested him myself, I panicked.

I whipped my head back, checking to see if the curtains of my house's front window moved. Did my parents hear his voice? He had to go. Less than two hours ago, my father had ripped into me for believing I was still associated with this man. He could not be here right now.

I jumped out of my seat, my hands coming out in front of me to usher him away from the front of my house. When my hands collided with his chest, rough in the way I pushed him away from the windows of my home, I did my best to ignore the jolt I felt in my stomach over the way his body felt firm under my fingers. I wasn't strong enough to get him to budge, so when he did create the necessary distance from my parents' house, it was because he took the steps back on his own.

"You can't be here!" I whispered, looking over my shoulder at my house warily. We were far enough away that I didn't need to speak so quietly, but anxiety was what made me speak in the urgent, hushed tones.

Kain didn't say anything at first, his expression neutral as his eyes seemed to explore everything about me in that minute-long silence. I swallowed hard, feeling goosebumps rise along the backs of my arms from the way his golden brown eyes shined bright and warm under the glow of a streetlight above.

"I was dropping something off," he replied simply, indicating it hadn't been his intention to run into me. I didn't like the way the realization made my insides twist with disappointment. He extended the bag in his hands my way. "Here."

I took a step back, offering up a refusal. "I don't want it."

"But it's yours," he informed, pushing it into my hands, sending an unexpected shiver down my back the second his fingers brushed against mine. I snatched my hand back, behaving as if his touch burned my skin. In that moment, however, I could've sworn it did. "It's the stuff you left at *Seven* last night."

Oh.

When my fingers closed around the bag's handle, Kain's right side cheek raised in a faint half smile. Something in my chest fluttered. I wondered if he could tell, because even after the bag was in my hands, he didn't turn and walk away. For a moment, he merely stood there, eyes on me in a way that should've made me feel self-conscious.

But these eyes were so familiar. Way too familiar to ever feel uncomfortable about them being on me. It was like the longer he stared, the further the fact that he'd betrayed me moved to the far corners of my mind. I was operating on a very here-and-now train of thought, not thinking about the past, not thinking about the future. I was here. And the moment was now.

So I didn't move either.

Did he feel the magnetic field in the foot-long space between us? Or was I imagining that?

"Have you been crying?" he asked quietly, finally ending the long silence we fell into.

And then I remembered the moments leading up to now. My father yelling at me in his office. Crying alone on the front porch. Did I even remember to wipe my face?

The space between Kain's eyebrows dipped, my only sign that he didn't like what he was seeing. In my peripheral vision, I saw the beginning of what looked like him raising his hand to touch me. He caught himself, though, ending the slow rise.

Kain made stopping himself look almost... painful.

"Why are you still here?" I whispered.

"Why are *you*?" he countered plainly, as if the five hundred and six days between us had passed like seconds. Kain, as always, was comfortable. Much more comfortable than I could ever hope to be given the history we had. He breathed with an unbothered ease as I forced myself to breathe through my nose, almost too conscious of the way my chest rose and fell rapidly while I stood before him. Did he notice how hard I was breathing? He spoke again, drawing me out of the semi-trance I floated in when he said, "Walk with me."

"I'm not going anywhere with you."

"Then we can stay here."

I looked over my shoulder, chewing on my lower lip nervously over the possibility of either one of my parents coming out of the house to check on me. If they found me whispering in the shadows with Kain Montgomery, it would just be another screaming match. I didn't have the energy to take another one of my father's screaming matches. Coming to that decision, I took the first step, walking past Kain a little, before he caught up and matched my stride.

"You wanna tell me why you were crying?" he asked as we passed the suburban two-stories that lined my quiet street. His tone could almost pass for concerned.

"No." I hated the way my heart beat so fast now, the way my body behaved as if this man meant something to me when I wanted so badly for him to mean nothing.

I could see Kain shake his head from the corner of my eye, a long exhale leaving him before he spoke again. "Yeah, you do."

I hated the way my body responded to the sound of his voice. My mind could try to not remember him, but from the way the hairs on my arms stood straight, the way my breathing could no longer keep pace, and the growing heat from between my legs—I just knew my body remembered him just fine.

Could he tell? If he could, did he feel powerful because of it?

The air that hung around us was somehow both familiar and tense at the same time. We were close together enough to notice we were close, and far enough apart for it to feel deliberate. Even though we spoke to one another as if no time had passed, time had clearly passed. Neither of us spoke as we walked side-by-side, breathing out clouds in the cool December night. I used to be so uncomfortable with silence. The anxiety it gave me would have me rush to fill empty space with words that didn't need to be said. Silence used to be intimidating.

Now, I found relief in it, thankful I didn't have to say anything anymore.

"Lauren—" I flinched, a visual representation of my heartbeat pausing for one deadly second. It had been so long since I'd heard my name said in that voice. There were parts of me that were convinced I'd never hear it again, and now those parts of me awoke at the exact moment he said the word, awakening my body with a visible jolt. Noting my reaction, Kain stopped what he was saying, and checked in. "You good?"

I was afraid of my voice sounding unconvincing, so I could only nod. And he nodded in response to this, accepting this as my truth. I took a step away, holding my breath as something in my chest waited for him to follow, waited for him to deny me the opportunity of creating distance.

Kain took a step to the side, keeping the six-inch space between us from getting any larger. I breathed out. It sounded relieved.

"Last night was..." He trailed off, unsure of what he should call it. "I just... I guess I just wanna know if you're gonna be alright."

What the hell did I say to him last night? Why is he behaving this way? From the bits and pieces I could remember from the night before, I knew Rashad made me cry last night. Did I tell Kain something about Rashad when I was drunk? Was that why he was still here, sounding all concerned about me?

Kain and I had met almost two years ago at a party where he stopped me from getting raped. If I'd gotten drunk last night and told him about the incident with Rashad, I could see why he would feel some type of way about it. All that trouble saving me last year, just for it to ultimately happen anyway.

"If this is about what I might've said about my boyfriend last night," I started to explain defensively, "just know that he doesn't always do that to me. You don't need to check up on me over it. It was one time and… it was kind of my fault 'cause I'd gotten him all horny, and… and it didn't even hurt. I don't need you popping up at my house, checking to see if I'm good."

Kain stopped walking.

"*What*?"

This was the tone of a man who was hearing all of this for the first time, blindsided. But that's not all he was. Understanding what I was implying, I watched calm and composed features morph into something resembling alarm.

Shit.

"Lauren, what do you *mean*?" Kain wasn't asking for clarification. Actually, he was more like pleading for some sort of indication that he'd misunderstood me. I'd misguidedly revealed the ugliest of bombshells, and now he stood before me, unable to mask the horror in his features. Kain's hands grasped at my shoulders tightly, facing me with urgency. "What *the fuck* do you mean?"

I shook my head vehemently, trying to shrug away his tight grip on me. Though, I couldn't shake him loose. Kain's hands held onto me firmly, unwilling to let me go in case I wanted to run from this.

"Why are you *yelling* at me?" I asked, feeling my squeaking voice shake. Did he think I did something wrong? Was he mad at me for it?

"You just told me that a nigga raped you! And you still callin' him your boyfriend after that?"

He was still shouting at me. I'd gotten enough of my fair share of being yelled at today. The volume of Kain's words grew, and between his hands, I shrunk.

I shook my head, feeling a pool form at the rims of my eyes. "Don't call it that."

"Call it what? *Rape*?" Still shouting, but not as loud.

My voice sounded tormented when I asked—begged—him to stop. "*Please* stop calling it that."

"Lauren," his voice hushed to a whisper, pulling me in closer by my shoulders. Kain sounded tormented as well when he whispered out the question, "Baby, what *happened* to you?"

I refused to be spoken to like I was broken.

"*Nothing* happened to me!" I shouted back, not looking him in the eyes. "It was *nothing*!"

"Like hell, nothing happened to you!" he retorted with infuriated sarcasm. He was so enraged, so angered over the realization of what Rashad had done to me. Seeing the ferocity burn in Kain's eyes did something to light up the anger within me as well.

"Don't stand there and act like you haven't done worse to me! You are such a hypocrite!" When confusion flashed in his features, I got to explaining. "Your father shot me! I almost died! I lost a lung! I lost our—" I shook my head, violently pushing him out of my face. "I lost so fucking much, Kain!"

Emotions on high, I didn't care that I was shouting in the quiet neighborhood.

"I lost so much," I repeated, bringing a hand to my face to wipe away the stray tears. "And you... You got up in front of millions of people, and defended the man who took so much from me! He tried to KILL me, and you still chose HIM!"

"Lauren—"

"Don't stand there and act like you're some king of caring about my wellbeing! I know he's your father, but," I shook with a sob, "he took *so much* from me. And you didn't even love me enough to just... choose me when I needed you the most."

Kain's eyes shined with the hint of tears. None of them fell, but the words coming out of my mouth were clearly dishing out emotional blows, making them form. Having never seen him like that before, my breath caught, and I took a step back.

His voice was calmer when he came to understand what I was saying. "You letting niggas abuse you because you measure them up against what you think I did."

"What I think you did?" I repeated, questioning his word choice. "Oh so now you're going to act like I'm stupid. Like I didn't hear about the testimony that ruined my father's career? Like I didn't spend two weeks on life support? Like I don't have the *scars* to prove it?!"

"You let niggas abuse you because you feel like it'll never be as bad as what you think I did to you." He seemed to only be focused on this fact. Kain sounded so... tortured.

"There's no man, no matter what they do to me, who will ever hurt me the way you did," I confirmed. Rashad might've raped me, but that was nothing compared to what Kain did.

Kain shook his head, a single drop gliding out from the inner corner of his eyes when he took another step closer to me. "There's so much about that night that you don't know."

"Oh really?" I hit back skeptically. "Like what?"

When Kain's hands drew up, taking my face between his palms, I thought he was going to kiss me as his face drew closer. Instead he simply pressed his forehead to mine, his breath hitting against my lips when he painfully replied, "I *can't* tell you."

I pushed him back, not caring if I was being rough.

"Of course you can't!" Why was I even surprised? "'Cause you're lying! That's what you do! You lie! You pretend to love me to draw me in, and when the time is right, you put me up for slaughter! You *never* loved me!"

"You don't believe that."

"What do you want me to believe?"

"You might believe a lot of things about me, Lauren, but I *know* you don't believe that."

"I don't know what to believe!" I shouted, taking a step back as he took a step forward. "I look into your eyes, and I just… I don't understand. I don't understand how you can look at me like that, knowing what you did!"

"What do you think I did?" he asked, matching my volume.

"Stop acting like you don't know!"

"I need to hear you say it!"

I was shouting at the top of my lungs now, hitting on his chest with every word I screamed.

"You. Protected. Him!" My body shook from both the emotions coursing through me, and the hurt in my heart. "He tried to kill me. And you protected him. You protected the man who tried to kill me."

Kain's hands took me by the shoulders, his eyes burning into mine when he slowly said the words. "No. I. Didn't."

"Liar!"

"Lauren," he stressed. "It *wasn't* Silas."

"Sure it wasn't." I was sarcastic. I had no idea I had so many murderous enemies running around. "Who was it then, Kain? Pray tell."

He drew in a sharp breath, ultimately shaking his head defeatedly when he, again, said the words, "I can't tell you." His hands on me griped tighter before I could push him away again. "It would destroy you."

I nodded, not buying his lies for one second. "Of course it would. That's what this is, huh? Some big plan to spare my feelings." I shook him off of me, thrusting another blow against his chest, hoping it would hurt him, but knowing it didn't when it landed. "I gave you everything! I gave you all of me! And you betrayed me! Yet somehow that's not as bad as whatever the real truth is. That's *bullshit*, Kain!"

"I'm serious," he stuck to his story.

"Well what if I don't care about *your* feelings?" I asked angrily, throwing a fist against his chest again, seriously wanting to hurt him. "What if I tell you something that destroys you? Will you tell me then? Will you tell me if I show you that I don't give a *shit* about how you feel?"

"Lauren—"

"Your father, who tried to kill me... That father that you love so fucking much..." I knew that what I was about to say, I could never take back. But, damn, I wanted to hurt him. I wanted to hurt him the way he let me hurt. I didn't have all the facts, but I didn't care. I just wanted him to break down the way that I had broken down dozens of times this past year. I wanted him to feel pain. "That father that you ride so hard for... Well, he..." I took a few steps back, already getting ready to head back home after I dropped this bomb. "He killed your mother."

Chapter Thirteen

KAIN

"Two times in less than thirty days," Silas said more to himself than he did to me, referring to the fact that this was the second time I'd visited him in less than a month. "You must be startin' to miss me."

I pulled out a metal seat, not saying anything when I took my seat across from him at the stainless steel table. My father's subtle smile faded, realizing this wasn't just some I-was-in-the-neighborhood type visit.

Making the drive down to the prison had been a long one, giving me a lot of time to think. I was taking walks down memory lane, remembering my childhood. As a child, my father had a really interesting way of spending time with me. Whenever I was with him, it always felt like I was there to learn something. He would explain the things he'd do, why he'd do them, and then open the floor for questions.

It was like having a devoted tutor, dedicated to making sure that I knew what it meant to be a Montgomery. Do this, not that. Say this, never that. Be here, not there. My father didn't believe in trivializing things to fit a child's frame of reference. He wouldn't talk down to me; he required me to simply keep up. If I had a question, Silas would answer it for me, always man-to-man even though I was clearly just a boy.

In hindsight, it was obvious that my upbringing wasn't much of a childhood.

I was four when I began to notice that my family dynamic was different than everyone else's. My sisters all had mothers. Sometimes they'd come around the house when they were there to pick someone up. As crazy as it sounds, in my four year old mind, I'd developed this sort of belief that only girls had moms. This was natural, though, because the only moms I'd ever met were my sisters' mothers.

I was in Memphis one summer with my uncle Vance. Silas might've been out of the country securing cartel connects or something. So I was with Vance that summer, living it up at my grandmother's house.

My grandmother was the toughest gangster I ever knew. She didn't kill anybody or carry a gun. In fact, it was rare to ever see her without a bible in her hands. Grandma was a gangster because, even at the age of four, I understood that she had something that no one else had. My grandmother was the only person I'd ever known who spoke to my father like he was... a child. It wasn't hard to see that somehow, that little old lady put the fear of God in Silas.

'Grandma.' That summer, I was four turning five, sitting at the kitchen table while she was making lunch. *'How come my Dad is scared of you?'*

She'd laughed at first, rubbing the top of my head with the palm of her hand and said, *'Oh, Tariq...'*

My grandmother called me by my middle name, never my first. She didn't like my first name. It had something to do with the bible, but I couldn't remember exactly what. All I knew was that in the bible, whoever was named Kain, was not a good person.

'My boys respect me, 'cause I'm they mama,' she'd explained simply, turning on the kitchen sink behind her and pulling up a basket from her garden.

I didn't understand. *'But only girls have moms.'*

'Who told you that?'

'Well, I don't have a mom,' I pointed out.

My grandmother had paused at first, turning away from the kitchen sink where she was rinsing greens, and just looked at me. I thought her eyes looked sad. *'Everybody has a mama, Tariq.'*

'Then where's mine?' I'd asked curiously just as my uncle Vance walked into the kitchen, having heard the private conversation. Something about my uncle's sudden presence had made my grandmother reel back. I could sense the conversation coming to a close even though I hadn't gotten any answers.

Grandma's eyes cut to Vance, and a look was held between the two of them. They knew something. Even at the age of four, I could tell that they knew something. And in that moment, they seemed to silently agree to not tell me what it was. When my grandmother's eyes came back to me, she'd walked over and crouched down so that we would be eye level.

'Your father will tell you one day,' she promised.

After that summer with my grandma in Memphis, I had gone back to Miami and the first thing I did when I saw Silas was ask him where my mother was. Silas had shaken his head and simply said, *'She ain't comin' back.'*

For years I took that to mean she'd left.

Silas was a hard person to be around, and it wasn't hard to imagine her just packing her things and leaving. I didn't miss her. How could I? I didn't even know her. Yeah, there was an empty feeling inside me for some time, feeling like a big part of who I was, was missing. But I didn't miss her. Over the years, observing the way my father treated the women in his life, I grew to appreciate the fact that wherever my mother was, she was far away from him.

There was a gnawing suspicion in me that something more sinister was hidden within the secrets of her whereabouts, but I didn't try to explore that. Part of me wanted to believe that she was off somewhere living her life; safe. So I didn't ask any questions that might diminish that belief.

"What's this all about?" Silas questioned, analyzing my face and realizing this wasn't some lighthearted visit.

I wasn't angry, nor was I all that grief-stricken. Again, if my mother was dead, it was all the same to me. I'd never known her. Most of the reason why I was here today was for the closure, a straight answer once and for all.

"Remember when I was five and I asked you where my mother was?" I asked first.

The space between my father's brows dipped, unsure of what direction I was trying to take us in. He took a moment to think about how he would proceed, his behavior giving no indication that he was distressed about being made to talk about this. Of course Silas would never falter and show me what he was really feeling. I was like that, too, and I'd learned to be that way by watching him.

"Did you kill her?" I didn't mince words—something else I learned from my father. All my life, I was taught to never beat around the bush when I wanted something. Silas used to say it all the time—real men don't ask, they demand.

"Where's all this comin' from?" he questioned.

When Lauren had dropped the ball on me the night before, it sounded like this was something about me that she'd known for quite some time. Sending me into a state of disbelief, her revelation had effectively ended the discussion, after which she turned around and ran home.

I didn't follow her.

It was never a good feeling to feel like you're the last to know something about yourself. I let her go because after she threw the information at me, clearly intending to inflict pain, I had nothing left to say. Lauren was hurting. I understood that. In her fragile temperament, she lashed out, throwing all the ammunition she had my way.

One hit landed.

Which was why I was here today, looking for answers.

"Just answer the question, Dad." I didn't come here to fight. If my mother was dead, then she had been for over twenty years, and nothing I said would change that. I just wanted answers. "Did you kill her?"

"Did someone tell you that?" Silas asked. "Who told you that?"

"So, you did kill her."

"No," my father denied it. Silas had very few reasons to lie to me about this. I would've believed him right then and there, but Lauren had sounded so sure. "It wasn't me," he said in a way that implied that while she was dead, he had no hand in it. "I didn't kill her."

"Someone did, though?" My father looked down at the stainless steel table between us, nodding his head solemnly. "Do I know them?"

Silas' shoulders fell, shaking his head as he replied, "The whole situation is a mess."

"What situation?"

"Kiana was a good kid," Silas informed. Was that her name? My father raised his gaze and affirmed, "She was real good. And she didn't deserve to go out like that. But it's... It's complicated, Kain."

I was losing my patience. "What the fuck happened?"

"Hey," Silas interjected sternly. "It's a lot of things that went down back in those days, but I'm still your Pops. Don't let nothin' anybody tells you make you forget that fact. I raised you on my own for years, and I will not sit here and have you cussin' at me like I'm some nigga off the street, you understand me?"

I couldn't tell if the subject was making my father sentimental, or if prison had really just simmered him down. Here he was, reprimanding me like I was sixteen again.

"Dad, I need answers."

"I didn't kill her," he stood firmly in that statement, meeting my eyes indignantly. I believed him. "It wasn't me."

"Then who?"

Silas forced out an exhale, eyes unblinking as he shook his head dejectedly. There was something lifechanging about the words he was getting himself ready to say. I could see it in the way he shifted in his seat uncomfortably, folding and unfolding his hands anxiously. When my father finally did speak again, his voice was apologetic, which was rare for him. "It was Vance."

* * *

The first thing Dr. Eloise said to me when I showed up for my noon appointment was, "What happened?"

Was what I'd been through this past weekend really that evident on my face?

"A lot," I replied, starting from Friday night at *Seven*, moving onto the Saturday evening argument with Lauren, and then finally my visit with Silas on Sunday. It had been a very eventful couple of days and by the time

Monday had rolled around... I was spent. "I haven't addressed it with my uncle yet."

I didn't know how. All my life, Vance was the one adult in my life that I felt had my best interests at heart. If what Silas had told me was to be believed—and I saw no reason for him to lie—then the Vance I knew was all a lie.

It was like multiple attacks were coming at me from different directions. There was the blame I took for Lauren's devaluing of herself. Then there was finding out that my mother was dead all this time. And lastly, finding out that the person who'd killed her was Vance, of all people... That one was the cherry on top of a shit sundae.

"Let's tackle the first one," Dr. Eloise went down the list of attacks. "Lauren devaluing herself. How is that your fault?"

"She accidently told me that the guy she's with has raped her before." I couldn't shake the intense anger that filled me every time I thought about it. It was the kind of anger that made me want to drive through Miami's bougiest neighborhoods and look for somebody named Rashad. "And in her mind, it's not even that bad 'cause it's nothing in comparison to what I did last year. Or... what she *thinks* I did."

"I see." Dr. Eloise took notes. "And this makes you feel like you're to blame."

"If not me, then who?" I asked.

"Why don't you tell me why you feel that way?"

"'Cause I thought that I..." This was hard to talk about. "I thought that it would be easier for her to heal if I stayed away. Lauren would've never been able to recover from the emotional damage of learning what really happened that night. But I could never be with her unless I told her. So I stayed away, not wanting to have to hurt her that way so I could keep her. My decision hurt her, I know, but it was necessary. I didn't realize, though, that by making that choice, I was setting her up to be accepting of men who don't treat her right. And it… it's my fault."

"And what does that make you feel like you need to do?" I couldn't answer Dr. Eloise's question because I didn't have an answer for her. I didn't know what to do anymore. My therapist tried to help me get there. "You let Lauren think you betrayed her because you thought that was what's best for her. This weekend you got to see the lasting effects of that decision. Answer me this, Kain, if this path of low self-worth and poor relationship choices is the path that she's on, are you not simply trading one negative effect for another? Lauren is… Lauren is…"

"She's fucked up either way," I finished her sentence. Finding Lauren sitting out on her front porch, crying alone on her birthday told me everything I needed to know about how good of a support system her family was. I thought if I left her alone, she could have that much needed relationship with her parents again.

I was wrong.

They let her suffer alone.

"And so let's talk about how she told you about your mother's death."

"She did that to hurt me."

"Was she successful?"

I shrugged, my answer was neither yes or no. Finding out my mother was dead didn't hurt me, finding out who killed her did. "Lauren's going through a lot. So she lashed out."

"That's very forgiving of you," my therapist acknowledged, bringing her pen to her teeth as she pondered for a moment. I shrugged, not seeing the meaningfulness that Dr. Eloise saw. Forgiving Lauren for her pain-fueled outrage was...easy. Dr. Eloise shook her head, a faint smile in her eyes as she declared, "Sometimes it's not the people who love us the most, or loved us first, that we need. Sometimes it's the people that love us the best." Her head tilted to the side. "You love her *so* much."

"Are you saying she needs me?"

Who would know this better than Lauren's own therapist? Of course, Dr. Eloise gave nothing away. Regardless of who paid for Lauren's sessions, patient-doctor confidentiality would always reign supreme.

Instead, Dr. Eloise asked for me to look for the answer inside myself. "What do you think, Kain?"

I didn't have an answer for her. The gray-haired woman leaned back in her seat, sensing that she was about to hit a wall with me as our session was coming to a close. She chose a less emotionally taxing topic to finish up the appointment with.

"So what's the word on Yale?"

Chapter Fourteen

Lauren

I didn't want to talk about my weekend with Dr. Eloise.

Yet somehow, without my saying so, she seemed to already know that this weekend had been a bad one for me. Sometimes I swore my therapist knew way more about me than she let on. She had motherly eyes, the same kind of eyes my mother would look at me with as a child when she knew I was doing something bad. It had a way of making me talk.

"I had another dream over the weekend," I told her. "Well… more like a nightmare."

"What happened?"

"I was standing at the edge of a really, really tall building. I was so close to the edge that the tips of my shoes hung off. If I even sneezed a little too hard, I would've fallen down the hundred stories to my death. But I was stuck at the edge."

"Did you want to jump?" Dr. Eloise asked.

"No," I replied. "It wasn't that kind of dream. It was like the last nightmare that I told you about. I felt like I was watching all of this go on from outside my body. I didn't feel anything. I didn't think anything. I just watched. And Kain was there, too."

"Was he crying in this one?"

"He wasn't… But he was sad, and he was whispering something in my ear. I don't know what, but I think he was trying to get me to step away from the edge. And then suddenly my dad appeared on the roof, too. The clouds got darker and it started to storm. The wind was blowing hard, strong enough to blow me off the edge of the building, but Kain's hand came up and caught me, and his hand settled right where my scar is."

Dr. Eloise wrote something down, nodding for me to continue.

"My dad yelled at him to stop touching me. Kain said, *'If I let her go, she'll fall.'* My dad didn't care, though. Dad said something about it costing too much money for me to stand on the roof, and that Kain either had to let me fall, or follow his instructions. It sounded like he was blackmailing him—using me. I don't understand what it means."

"There's a lot to unpack here." Dr. Eloise set her pen down on her notepad, leaning forward when she asked, "What did you feel when you woke up?"

"Scared."

"Why scared?"

I shivered a little. "Because… Because nothing like that has ever happened to me in real life, but… but it didn't feel like a dream," I explained, chewing on my bottom lip anxiously. "It felt like a memory."

"Have your father and Kain Montgomery every been in the same place at the same time before?"

"Only once," I remembered. "When we first started dating, it happened one night... and it was all kind of downhill from there."

"Was there anything that happened over the weekend that you feel would make these kinds of dreams occur?" There she went again asking me questions as if she was getting insider information from somewhere else. "It was your birthday on Saturday, correct? What did you do for your birthday?"

"I don't really want to talk about it," I mumbled.

"I can't help you if you don't talk to me Lauren."

I felt embarrassed all of a sudden. My twenty-first birthday had been shamefully bad. Starting with my fight with Rashad, then my fight with my father, and then lastly the fight with Kain. I'd run to my bedroom after that last argument, casting the bag that Kain had dropped off, and cried for at least two hours. It wasn't until Morgan got home from celebrating with her friends that somebody thought to check on me.

I told my sister what I could, barely going into detail, focusing mostly on the actions of our father that day. Morgan sat on my bed beside me and wrapped an arm around my shoulders. *'Lauren, there's something I have to tell you,'* she'd whispered. *'I think you'll stop letting the way Daddy treats you affect you so much if I tell you this.'*

'What is it, Morgan?' I had replied in a whisper.

'The night you woke up…' Morgan's eyes began to water, which told me that whatever she was about to say had to be painful. Morgan never cries. *'Mom and Dad were already at the hospital the night you woke up, but it's not because they were there to visit you…'* My sister shifted uncomfortably in her seat beside me before she revealed, *'They were there to cut off your life support.'*

'They made me swear I'd never tell you,' Morgan had informed. *'But can I be honest with you? After your ex embarrassed him earlier that day, he came home so angry. He just up and decided to cut off your life support that day, but it felt like… It felt like it was in retaliation to something. It was like Daddy suddenly wanted to take you off the breathing machine because Kain Montgomery had made a fool of him. It was like he was getting revenge.'*

My sister went on to explain even more. *'Mom protested. I don't want you to think she didn't fight for you, but Dad made it a money thing and brought up the fact that he'd just lost his job, and that we really couldn't afford to keep you in the hospital anymore. He was so ready to let you die, Lauren. When the machines were turned off, however, you started breathing on your own. And that's the only reason you're still with us. So, stop looking at Daddy like you expect him to grow a heart and start acting like he cares. Daddy only cares about himself. You don't need to cry over him.'*

Dr. Eloise reached for a few tissues on her desk, handing them to me as I finished up with telling her the story I was told.

"And that's the dream you had after your sister told you all of that," my therapist gathered. "Well the dream makes sense, then. You have a sister who tells you that your father wanted to cut off your life support, the same night, you have a dream about your father wanting to cut your life support. In a symbolic way. In the dream, Kain was your life support."

"No..." I whispered. "That's not the part that scared me. In the dream, my father was blackmailing him and using me as leverage. And for some reason, it felt like this was something I had witnessed before."

"When was the last time you saw Kain?" my doctor asked.

"Last year," I lied.

She eyed me as if she automatically knew that was a lie, but she didn't press harder. I don't know why, but I was ashamed of the truth. I'd seen Kain less than forty-eight hours ago. He'd stopped by to drop off a bag with the stuff I'd left at *Seven*. When I took it, I had just assumed that was all that would be in there. This was not the case, however.

In the bag he'd dropped off, my purse was inside, of course, but there was one more thing inside as well. A red and gold jewelry box with the word *Cartier* written across the top in beautiful script. A birthday gift. The only one I'd received that day. When I'd opened the box, a beautiful gold bangle was nestled between a velvety pocket. He had a custom engravement written on the inside.

With love. Always. -K

I'd wanted to throw it away so bad, shoving the box back in the bag it'd come in, and walking to my trash bin. But my fingers would not allow me to drop the gift inside. I didn't want it. I didn't want anything from him.

But I couldn't throw it away.

Again, I'd taken the bracelet out of its packaging, bringing it closer to my face and reading the inscription over a dozen more times.

With love.

With love...

Love...

I hated him. I hated him so much for having such a big piece of me. I hated that I went to sleep thinking about him that night, and I hated that he was still on my mind when I awoke the following morning. I hated that when he was close, I could feel myself drawing closer to him as if I couldn't help myself.

God, I missed him.

And I hated myself for it.

Dr. Eloise did not seem pleased with me and my unwillingness to be honest with her, but as our uneventful session drew to a close, all she could do was eye me disapprovingly. Just like my mother might. I met her stare head on, ready to ride out the last five minutes of our session in awkward silence. It was she who ultimately gave in. She needed to remind me that I didn't have a session next week.

"As you know, next Monday is Christmas Day, so—"

"So my appointment is moved to Tuesday at three, I remember."

My therapist nodded, reaching into the distance that separated us to lay a hand on my shoulder. The touch was gently, meant to convey an air of compassion. Her parting words for me were, "At some point, you're going to have to open up, sweetheart."

"I'll try harder next time."

The sky was cloudy when I stepped outside. Distracted, I was digging in my purse for the keys to my car, getting ready to get on with my day. Talking to Dr. Eloise had reminded me that I had a week until Christmas and I'd yet to buy anyone in my family gifts.

Had it not been for the inscription he'd added, I might've been able to get away with giving the bracelet Kain had gifted me to Morgan. She would go nuts if she got a real *Cartier* Love Bracelet.

I checked the time on my phone, determining that I had about three hours until the mall closed. There, I could get everyone some cost effective kiosk gift and then cross Christmas shopping off my to-do list. Checking the time on my phone also allowed me to see that I had two new text messages—both from Rashad. I hadn't spoken to him in more than two days, the last time we spoke being that night at Seven.

Rolling my eyes, I pulled up his contact profile and pressed down on the screen for a call. It rang twice before he picked up in a frenzy. He sounded surprised to be hearing from me.

"Lauren!" There was relief in his greeting. Perhaps he thought I was never going to call him, and he was relieved to have been wrong.

"Hey, Rashad, I'm—" I didn't get my chance to apologize to him for the weekend-long silence. The moment I said his name, a hand reached up from behind me and pulled the phone away from my ear. After what I told Dr. Eloise about Rashad last week, I half expected her to be standing behind me, taking my phone away from me for what she believed was my own good.

I turned on my heel to confront the small, older woman. If I wasn't in her office, she had no right to butt into my life. I was already in a bad mood.

Upon turning, it took me a fraction of a second to realize that the person behind me was neither small, or a woman. My eyes traveled up an athletically built body, rising up along a dark wash pair of jeans, a long-sleeved white Henley shirt, and then ultimately a pair of eyes. Staring back at me were a familiar set of golden brown eyes, and I felt my insides twist. *Is he following me now? How did he know I was here?*

Rashad shouted hellos from my phone, asking where I'd gone. "Lauren, are you there? Lauren, hello?"

Kain, just before he hung up the phone, put the receiver to his mouth, and aggressively let my boyfriend know, "She's busy."

Chapter Fifteen

KAIN

When Lauren gets angry, she breathes faster.

A pinch will form between her brows, her lips will press into a hard line, and her voice gets one pitch higher. At least, that's what I could remember. The New Lauren, the one I hadn't been around for sixteen months, she added one more thing to the mix.

Hands.

The New Lauren hits when she's angry. Was that just for me? Or was she really out in these streets picking fights I knew her weak ass hands would not be able to back up? Her punches landed onto my body like nothing, and as her sixth one connected, I actually thought to myself, *Damn, I gotta teach her how to fight...*

"Give me back my phone!" she shouted, but then stopped, her eyes widening as she scanned the space around us. It seemed to dawn on her then that she couldn't be seen with me in public. Couldn't get caught with a Montgomery with her ain't-shit father was running for governor and all. When she demanded her phone again, she spoke in harsh whispers. "Give me back my phone!"

"No," I countered, stuffing the rose gold phone down my back pocket. She wasn't getting this back until we talked. "We didn't get to finish our conversation from the night before."

"Are you here to yell at me again?"

"The only person yellin' right now is you."

She shook her head, her arms coming out to cross in front of her chest. Lauren spoke a little more quietly when she urgently asked, "How did you even know I was here? Are you following me now?"

"No."

"Then how did you know that I'd be he—"

"It's a long story," I interjected, not really feeling like now was the time to let her know that I was the one who was paying for her therapy. "There was something you said Saturday night that we need to talk about."

"I don't want to talk to you."

"Okay," I nodded, acknowledging her request even though, this time, I wasn't going to respect it. "But we still gon' talk, though."

"If I get photographed with you again, my dad will kill me." That didn't feel like a figure of speech in Lauren's case. She had nothing to worry about, though.

"Photographers don't hang around the outside of health offices." *I'm pretty sure that's illegal.* "We need to talk about you feeling like I set you up."

"What's there to talk about?"

"That's not what happened, but I think you know that." I came forward, and she took a step back. I could see it in her eyes that the closer I got, the weaker her resolve became. It wasn't my intention to will her into submission, though. I didn't want Lauren to give in to me because I persuaded her to. I wanted her to give in to me because it was something she wanted. "On Saturday night you said I never loved you. Do you really feel that way?"

"Someone who loved me wouldn't have done the things that you did."

"I don't think you realize the full extent of the things that I've done."

Lauren rolled her eyes, visibly irritated with this conversation. "You think because you buy me a bracelet, I'm supposed to have some sort of epiphany like *'Oh, I guess he does love me after all.'* It's not that easy! You have no idea what your father took from me!"

She was misunderstanding me, but it would be very difficult to plead my case without inflicting more damage. Somewhere in there, behind those combative eyes, was a heartbroken woman who longed for an explanation I couldn't give. It was hard to stand there and watch the tears form at the rims of her eyes. I was asking for the near impossible. I was asking for a woman to ignore the blaring facts before her eyes and take me at my word.

Ignore what you see and simply believe me…

That was a lot to ask.

Lauren was not the kind of girl to be so malleable. She wouldn't believe me just because I asked her to. I liked that about her, but it left me at a loss for options. It was do or die at this point, and no matter how apprehensive I was about shattering her perception of her father, I had to acknowledge the fact that was whether I told Lauren or not... she was going to feel pain.

It had been my assumption that it would be better for her to simply believe I betrayed her. Because then at least she'd have an entire family for support. But I was wrong. Her family seemed to be adding onto the pain that she already felt. At least if it were me tasked with the job of being her support, I'd actually do it.

As Dr. Eloise said, sometimes it's not the people who love you more, or love you longest, that you need in your life. Sometimes it's the people who love you in the best way. I may not have loved Lauren the most or the longest, but lately I was convinced I loved her best.

"Lauren—"

"You have no idea what I lost," she cut me off. "I lost..."

Her voice broke before she could finish her statement, her chest heaving as she pushed back a sob. Without her saying so, I automatically knew Lauren was referring to the baby that we'd lost.

If there was ever any question in my mind as to whether Lauren knew about her pregnancy before she was shot, there wasn't anymore. She knew. Clear as day, Lauren's pain was that of a woman who'd lost a baby she'd already begun to envision.

I might've mourned the loss of a child that could've been, but Lauren was mourning a child that already was. I lost my resolve. Lauren was already falling to pieces in front of me, and no amount of talking myself into it would allow me to pile onto her overwhelming pain. You don't watch your girl grieve the loss of your child and add on to the trauma by saying, '*By the way, your dad shot you by accident, and then threatened to kill you on purpose.*'

I couldn't fucking do it.

Instead, I reached into the distance between us and pulled her in closer, tucking her head just below my chin. Initially, she tensed up and I drew in a breath as I prepared myself for the emotional blow of being pushed away. She didn't do that, however. I couldn't tell if this was because she felt secure in my arms or if this was because she had no more fight left in her. Lauren simply leaned her forehead onto the raised structure of my collarbone and cried, the feel of her tears like acid on my skin.

"I know," I whispered.

She wasn't sure she'd heard me correctly. "You *know*?"

Gently, I pulled back so that I could get a better look at her face, running my thumb across the trail of tears on her cheek. She looked at me, eyes asking for clarification. She didn't understand.

"I was there," I confessed. "I was at the hospital, by your bedside, the morning it happened." I found out about the pregnancy and the miscarriage both in the same second. It was... *fucked up*, to say the least.

Lauren's eyebrows came together confusedly, almost angrily. "You were there?"

I only nodded. Her hands came up roughly, and she pushed me away.

"You mean to tell me that, you witnessed my disfigured body miscarry my baby as a *direct* result of the fact *your* father ordered someone to shoot me in the fucking chest, and then—if I have my dates correct—no more than forty-eight hours later, you took the stand and did everything possible to make sure Silas walked? Despite what he did to me?" The tears in her eyes created a sharp contrast with the rage in her voice. "I tried to be realistic, you know? He's your dad and you care about him. I get that. How could I ever expect you to love me more than your own father? But..." Her chest heaved with another sob, and she slammed a closed fist between her breasts as though trying to dull the pain of her heart breaking. "Your baby. *Our* baby. He took that from me, and you knew. And you still let him—"

"Lauren," I said her name like a plea, as if listening to this was pure torture. But that's because it was torture. "Think about what you're saying to me. Who do you think I am?"

"I don't know!" she shouted back at me. "I *don't* know anymore! I thought I knew, but now I'm so confused. It doesn't make any sense. None of this makes any sense!"

Agreeing, I replied, "It doesn't. So what does that tell you?"

She grew frustrated. "What do you mean, so what does—"

"It doesn't make sense because it's not true! You *really* think if Silas was the reason we lost our baby I would've taken up for him? You're right, that shit don't make sense at all, and that's because it's not fuckin' true!"

Lauren wiped at her cheeks, stunned into silence. My words were sincere, and I could tell that she needed a moment to think about what I was saying. She eyed me very analytically scanned my features for signs of dishonesty. I knew she wouldn't find any. I watched as a half-dozen emotions hit her at once. Shock, confusion, skepticism, and most surprisingly—*relief*. It was as if this was the moment she'd desperately needed, but even then, she wouldn't let herself give in. Her expression hardened.

"So what's the truth?" she questioned. "Please explain some sense into this… this… *fucked up* situation."

She waited for me to speak. Soaking in the moment, I seriously considered telling her the awful truth. I wondered what it would do to her emotionally to learn that her father was the culprit. Did I have it in me to tell her that her own father pulled the trigger, and after realizing what he'd done, he still tried to use it to get ahead? I thought about the deep wounds of betrayal the truth would leave. Twenty years would go by and she would likely still never completely get over it. Would I be able to mitigate the damage done? Would I even be given the opportunity?

A woman can overcome a broken heart. I imagine it comes with a lot of self-blaming. '*I picked the wrong one,*' kind of thoughts, probably. And then one day, like with all heartache, it doesn't hurt as much. They move on, and they learn from the experience.

What is there to learn from the realization that your father could give a fuck about you if it meant his career was on the line?

Breaking Lauren's heart was the hardest thing I ever had to do. I hated the way she looked at me now—like she wasn't sure she knew me. I could make it all go away right now. I could tell her the truth, and let her father be the one on the receiving end of her distrustful eyes.

But then I'd be breaking her heart all over again, breaking it in ways I was sure I'd never be able to fix. It's well understood that a woman can overcome a broken heart when it comes from a lover. It'll take time, but she may eventually rise above the damage, renewed and ready to tackle whatever life throws at her next. It makes her stronger. But the kind of pain that comes from a father's betrayal? There's nothing to learn in that. That shit will stay with her forever. It will not make her stronger.

"I can't," I said resignedly. "I really can't."

"Of course!" She let out a frustrated sigh. "What? Is it some big, bad Montgomery family secret? Huh? You used to tell me secrets all the time. Remember, Kain?" A few tears pooled at the rims of her eyes, falling as she continued to shout at me. "Remember how you used to tell me I was special? Remember that first morning we went all the way, and you told me you were mine forever? Was that real? Did you *ever* love me? You never said it. I had to ask you! Only then did you confirm, but you never said it outright. Don't think I didn't notice. You avoided the word like it was some kind of disease. You never loved m—"

"Yes, I did!" I matched her volume, startling her just a little. Shaking my head, I closed my eyes to force back the water I felt forming in them. When I opened my eyes, I confessed, "And I told you often. I slept in that hospital room for two weeks straight. It was the first thing I'd tell you every night, as I came in, and the last thing I told you every morning, before I left."

She said nothing as she processed the revelation.

"Lauren, I still—"

"Two weeks," she interrupted, doing the math. "I was asleep for two weeks and two days. I miscarried in the morning, two days before I woke up. You were there, right? You said you were. Was that when you decided to leave me and not come back? Were you mad at me for getting pregnant? Is that why you—"

"Don't even finish that question," I warned. It was clear where she was going, and it couldn't have been further from the truth. "No... No, I wasn't mad at you for getting pregnant."

I was offended that she'd even imply that I was capable of something so disgusting. Like I would try to punish her for wanting to have my child. If it were up to me, I would've never left that hospital room. She had no idea what I was up against that summer.

"I stayed that morning," I revealed. "Every day before that, when visitation hours kicked in, I made sure I got my ass out of that hospital room before either of your parents showed up and called security again. Not that morning. That morning, no one was gonna make me leave. Lauren... I was a fuckin' *mess*.

"Do you remember that night after Amir's funeral, and you noticed I didn't cry? You said my emotions were gonna catch up with me and I wasn't gonna know how to deal with it. After you were shot, I shed tears for the first time in almost ten years, but I kept it together. I thought that was the worst of it. I thought you had it all wrong about my emotions catchin' up with me.

"I kept it together for thirteen days, holding onto the belief that you would wake up, recover, and we would be alright. I kept it together because I hadn't lost you yet. And that kept me grounded; it kept me sane. And then I woke up one morning, and discovered you had been pregnant with my... *our* baby – and that we'd lost it. All in the same sentence. And I'm not mad at you for getting pregnant, but *goddamn*... That was a really fucked up way to find out.

"And for that, the last shred of composure I had left... *Gone*. I did not know how to deal with that loss of control. My emotions finally caught up with me, and I felt *everything*. All at once. Every emotion I'd ever bottled up—from the pain of losing my grandmother when I was fuckin' thirteen, all the way to that moment when I learned we lost our baby… Every emotion I'd ever suppressed between those two moments in time hit me all at once. And I *cracked*. I shut down.

"Later your father stopped by your hospital room, having already been briefed about your miscarriage, and when he found me there, he…" I sighed. "Let's just say it was a conversation I'm glad you didn't have to hear. I was put in this position where I had to choose—it was either you or Silas, and it may not look like it from where you stand, but believe me when I say, I chose *you*. I was gonna to get on the stand and testify against my own father. That may not seem like much to you, but that's a damn death wish where I come from. And then a few hours before I took the stand, I found out…"

I looked into her eyes and for the second time in my adult life, I felt helpless. She waited for me to finish, but I just couldn't do it. I couldn't tell her the truth.

All I said was, "Silas had nothing to do with you gettin' shot that night."

Lauren seemed to snap out of the trance I held her in, her eyes rolling incredulously at my admission.

"Oh," she nodded sarcastically. "I didn't realize I had so many violent enemies. You mind telling me who else it could've been?"

"I *can't*."

"Yes, you can! You don't want to!"

She was absolutely right about that. I'd sooner take a bullet to the chest before I ever dished out the kind of pain telling her the truth would cause.

"Do you trust me?" I asked.

"I trusted you—"

"No," I interrupted. "I'm asking you about right now. Look at me and tell me if you trust me or not."

She struggled with the words on the tip of her tongue, holding them back like they were desperate to escape, and she needed to keep them in. "I don't…" she cried, swiping the back of her hand along the tears falling down her cheeks. "I don't… I don't know."

"You do know," I told her. "Why else would you seriously be askin' me about that night, so ready to take my word for it, when I have every reason to lie? Do you *trust* me?"

"I hate you," she squeaked out, but not in a way that expressed that she meant it. It was a concession, a white flag before she finally admitted, "I hate that I still do. I trust you."

Relief blanketed my chest. Somewhere in there, somewhere behind that defensive attitude and those leery eyes… my girl was still in there. I took a step forward, not audacious enough to touch her again just yet, but close enough that it established an air of intimacy.

"Believe me when I say I can't tell you."

She bowed her head, pushing out a breath as though she was exhausted. Without warning, Lauren leaned in a little closer, taking me by surprise when her forehead pressed against my collarbone, just above my chest. In the quiet of the moment, all I could hear were the sounds of her sniffing and breathing. When my hand came up around her, she shook a little less, relaxing into my embrace.

"Did I ever love you?" I brought back her original question. "Baby, I never stopped."

Chapter Sixteen

KAIN

I didn't want to let her go home.

Being with Lauren now was like last spring all over again, finding hiding places in order to be around her. Except now she was the only one who was apprehensive about being seen with me.

She was here, though.

I knew that it was difficult for Lauren to take me at my word on such a serious issue, so it wasn't surprising that she wasn't all the way comfortable in my presence. But evidently, she didn't want to go home either. Lauren sat in the passenger's seat of my car, propping an elbow on the passenger's side window with her head resting on her hand. She was staring at me.

"What?"

"How did you know that I was here?"

I didn't think now was the time to tell her that I was the one who'd been paying for her therapy all this time, so I simply replied, "We have the same therapist."

This wasn't exactly a lie. It just wasn't a full answer.

"You're in therapy?"

"Yeah," I confessed, reminding her that it had been her suggestion almost a year and a half ago. "I made you a promise when you were in the hospital. I said that if you woke up I'd start going. I also said that if you woke up—"

"You would do whatever I wanted," she finished my sentence, which quite frankly scared the shit out of me. "That's what you said, right?"

"Yeah, I said that, too," I confirmed with an air of caution. This was only something Lauren would've known if she was coherent in her coma. Curiously, I questioned, "Were you able to hear what was going on in the room around you when you were in the hospital?"

Quickly, she shook her head, telling me she didn't know. When I asked how she guessed, she got a sheepish look about her, like her answer was something that embarrassed her.

"Sometimes, I dream about you," she admitted. "For the longest time I wondered where they were coming from, and why they feel like memories, and not dreams... but... I had this dream once of you telling me that I was right about you needing therapy, and then you said you'd get it if I asked. Then you added onto that and said you'd do whatever I wanted if I could just find the voice to ask. I didn't know what it meant, but... you were sad. You were always sad in my dreams."

Hearing this made me nervous. All this time spent trying to protect Lauren from the truth about her father, and the truth might've been hidden in her subconscious mind all along. I pressed her for more details. "Are those dreams common?"

"More or less. Sometimes they're just of us talking. I've had dreams about conversations with you. You'd just talk and talk and talk, but I rarely ever responded. You would tell me things; things you've never told anyone, you said. Like how everyone thinks you're going to University of Miami for law school, but that you actually want to go to Yale if you can get in. Is that true?"

Damn, she really did hear me... "Yeah... Yeah, that's true."

"I once had this dream where you were talking about... the baby. You told me that you weren't mad at me, and shared that you actually wanted a family of your own." A single tear rolled down her cheek as she continued. "And that both of us would've meant the world to you. Did you say that to me when I was in the hospital?"

Whatever it was that made Lauren so emotional all the damn time was clearly contagious. "Yeah, I said that, too."

There was a pause in the back and forth, Lauren lost in thought, and me sitting on the edge of my seat, nervous about what she'd bring up next. Whatever it was that was on her mind, it dulled the energy around her, it made her pause. She wasn't sure she wanted an answer to her next question.

"Did my dad ever threaten you before, Kain?" she asked finally.

"Lauren…"

"Was there ever a moment where he made you feel like if you didn't do something for him, he was going to let me die? Is that what you meant when you said you chose me?" I suppose my silence was all the answer she needed for those questions. "That's how he got you in court that day, huh?"

I was at a loss for words.

How could I have ever forgotten how smart the girl in front of me was? Lauren didn't seem surprised as she forcibly brought these truths to light. It made me wonder how badly her father had been treating her this past year for her to even see these situations within the realm of possibility.

"Is that the big secret?" she asked. "'Cause if it is, then let me be the first to tell you that he actually made good on his threat after your show at the courthouse that day. The night I started breathing on my own… According to my sister, I only started breathing on my own because him and my mom had personally gone to the hospital to have me taken off the machines." She looked away from me, her eyes, angry, and glancing out the window. "They were ready to let me die, Kain."

Her voice broke with the last statement, and upon hearing the hurt in her words, something in me broke too. I'd worked so hard to keep her from ever finding out about this, and here she was, putting together all the pieces on her own. I reached over and pulled her in, her body sliding over the car's center console until she was far into my embrace. Unlike the times I'd attempted to hold her, she didn't tense up or push me away. Instead, Lauren pressed her face into my chest, and as quietly as she could, she cried for a very long time.

"So that's what you were trying to protect me from finding out," she whispered conclusively, head rising away from my chest to look up at me. Her eyes were pink and her cheeks were wet. She waited for me to give her some sort of confirmation.

"Part of it."

"There's more?" She sounded worried, scared to hear what else there might be. It painfully twisted my insides. There was still the truth behind how she even ended up in that hospital bed, the truth behind who shot her.

"Lauren, it gets so much worse."

I felt her cringe under me.

"I want to know," she asserted. "Just 'cause I cry, doesn't mean I can't handle the truth. I'm not the person I was last year. I'm strong now."

With a shake of my head, I let her know, "Baby, you've always been strong."

Not many people could go through all the things that Lauren had been through and still get back up and essentially ask for more. She spent months dodging the murderous promises of my father with a smile on her face. She took a bullet, lost an organ, miscarried, and spent more than a year with the belief that a man who said he loved her betrayed her. And here she was, a little different than the woman I remembered, but for the most part, barely changed. She had to be one of the strongest people I knew.

"So... on a scale of one to ten, how bad is the whole truth?"

"Twenty."

She nodded, releasing a slow and calming breath.

"I can take it." And she wasn't bluffing. Her eyes zeroed in, and I could tell that she was bracing herself. She seemed ready, but was I? I guess I needed to be. However, just as I prepared to honor her request, she stopped me. "Wait. Could you tell me next week, on Monday night?"

"That's oddly specific."

"The truth..." she paused, her front teeth sinking into her lower lip nervously. "It'll change everything, won't it?"

I was honest with her. "Yeah."

"Maybe it's best I hear it after Christmas Day." She broke eye contact, looking down at her lap self-consciously. "That probably sounds so stupid, but—"

"It doesn't sound stupid." I tucked a finger under her chin, drawing her head back up so that she could meet my eyes. Her sienna brown skin took on blueish tones under the darkening sky outside. It was getting late, and as much as I would've liked to take her home with me, I knew she'd need some time. Honestly, after the past few days that we had, we both needed some time.

Even if it was what we wanted, nothing could ever just jump back to normal out of sheer desire for it to.

Things like this took effort, relearning, and time. Lauren's face inches from mine could've felt like the most natural thing in the world, but I already knew that emotionally we might've been miles apart. I ran my thumb repetitively along her cheek, my mind unable to recall the last time I got to touch her like this. Lauren leaned further into my hands, the space between our lips shrinking to a single centimeter.

I could've kissed her right then. The permission was in the way she closed her eyes and seemed to wait for me to close that final gap. I thought I might hate myself for the decision I made, but I pulled back. "I'll see you Monday night."

Chapter Seventeen

KAIN

I never liked Christmas.

There's this age old belief that the worst person to buy gifts for is a person who has everything. All my life, come holidays like Christmas, people loved to make excuses for their clearly last minute gifts, by saying things like, *'Well, Kain, you have everything.'*

Did I, though?

I was at Sanaa's today.

Sanaa *loved* Christmas.

Well, actually, Sanaa loved any occasion she could throw a party for. This year, however, she wasn't throwing a Christmas party. My guess was that this was because our father wasn't going to be here this year. The holidays last year had a way of making the fact that Silas was locked up more real to my sisters. They'd skipped out on grand gestures for the past two holiday seasons.

Thanksgiving dinner at Monique's last month had been smaller in comparison to the previous years. Less people were invited, and less effort went into planning.

Even considering the already small guest list, eleven people just "forgot" to show up—myself included. I had the excuse of being at the prison that night, but the other ten people just didn't feel compelled to come if Silas wasn't going to be there.

That's the way things were going to be now.

Not that my father was ever the life of any party. It's just that people in our extended family took invitations from him more seriously. Nobody wanted to be the person who Silas called up the next day, offended, because they'd missed one of his daughters' holiday parties. I guess it could be said that when it came to the whole family—uncles, aunts, cousins—Silas was the glue that kept them together. Or, more appropriately, he was the threat that kept them in line.

Christmas this year, as usual, was at Sanaa's. She didn't let the smaller guest list keep her from being extra. The house was decked out in multiple shades of red and green, and she'd said the word "festive" at least thirty-one times since I got here this morning. In attendance this year were my other two older sisters, Cierra and Monique. Monique brought her family. Cierra brought her attitude. And I brought impatience.

We didn't get each other gifts in my family.

We'd stopped all that when I was about fifteen because it got to be predictable. Every year until the day we stopped, I would get all of my sister's gift cards, Monique would get everyone something personalized and heartfelt, Sanaa would get everyone exactly what they wanted, and Cierra would give everyone slightly less attitude than usual. Christmas morning would always end with Monique feeling some kind of way because Sanaa's gifts were better received than hers.

So we just stopped.

It was half-passed noon when Sanaa caught me checking my watch for the hundredth time that day.

"You got someplace to be, K?"

If she was trying to shame me for coming off uninterested, it didn't work. "Yeah, I do."

"You meeting up with a girl?" Cierra asked curiously. Over the past year and a half, our relationship operated on a fine mix of cordial and tolerance. Every once and a while, she'd be neither and actually take interest. It might take years for Cierra and I to get to the way we were before, but we weren't as bad as we were last year.

When I didn't deny it right away, Sanaa immediately perked up. "Ooh, and who might that be?"

"You guys, leave Kain alone," Monique encouraged. I could think of a couple reasons why Monique would want to avoid discussing anyone I might be seeing. The last time she got involved with one of my relationships, she was dubbed an accomplice to a murder plot.

"It's not Eden, is it?" Cierra asked, her face twisting up like she was grossed out.

"Ewwuh," Sanaa interjected, denying the relationship for me. "Eden is practically family. Besides... Kain *clearly* has a type."

I checked my watch again. Damn, only six minutes had gone by.

"You got a lil' Christmas date with a lady scheduled? You could double date with me and Micah," Sanaa offered, not only to be nice, but because her ass was nosy and she wanted to be introduced.

Little did Sanaa know that her boyfriend, Micah, had visited Silas in prison months ago, asking for his blessing. I only knew this because Silas told Vance, and Vance told me in October. The proposal had yet to come even though Sanaa's birthday had come and gone in the first week of December. One could only assume that Micah was saving the question for Christmas or New Years.

Either way, I wasn't trying to be there.

"I pass."

"You must not like her all that much, then," Sanaa concluded immediately. "When you like a girl, you bring her around."

"What are you even basing that off of?" Monique squinted at Sanaa, as if to say there wasn't nearly enough evidence to back up that claim. "Kain has only ever brought around one girl."

"Yeah, I know," my sister nodded, placing her hand on her heart thoughtfully. "And she was my *best* friend."

Sanaa was definitely one for the theatrics.

"Oh, please." Cierra rolled her eyes. "That girl was not your best friend, Sanaa."

Sanaa met Cierra's face with a scowl, throwing up a hand for her to talk to.

"Well, now she's *nobody's* friend 'cause you told Daddy about her, and he had somebody *shoot* her," Sanaa countered, effectively killing the mood. Cierra looked down at her lap, the slightest bit of guilt crossing her features. It got quiet. Sanaa was still irritated, clearly still not over about what happened to Lauren last year.

None of my sisters knew what I knew. Like everyone else, they bought into the story that Lauren's shooting had something to do with Silas. The evidence lined up too well for it to have not been Silas.

The actual truth was a very hard to believe story. Given the choice between Lauren's father and Silas, no one would ever not assume Silas. Maybe I could've tried a little harder to get the word out, but—being completely honest—there was a very small part of me that liked my father better behind bars. I don't think I was the only one who felt that way. Even though Vance knew the truth as well, it didn't escape my notice that he wasn't talking either.

Silas spent his days locked away, awaiting trial for a crime he didn't commit. Though, in the grand scheme of things, it was nothing compared to the time he never served for the crimes he did commit.

I wondered if Vance kept quiet as a form of quiet revenge. After spending twelve years in prison for a crime that Silas committed, it wasn't shocking that Vance wasn't doing everything he could to see Silas freed.

In light of new information, though, I no longer felt sorry for the years Vance spent in prison. If Silas' words about who killed my mother were to be believed, Vance got off easy in life with the time he'd served. At least now I knew what Silas used to get his brother to confess to his crime.

I wasn't angry as much as I was disillusioned. I couldn't say this enough—I didn't know my mother. For me to get enraged over the possibility that Vance might've killed her just wasn't realistic. What the new information did do, however, was make it very hard for me to look at my uncle the same way. I hadn't spoken to him in days, and I didn't have plans on getting in touch any time soon.

I checked my watch again. Only fifteen minutes had gone by. Today was going to be a long one.

* * *

Lauren

When I was a little girl, I used to love Christmas.

Christmas used to be one of the only days of the year where my sister and I had the full attention of my mom and dad. Mom would put away her teacher hat, Dad would stop talking about convictions for a change, and we would all just wake up early and spend the whole day as a family.

Last year's Christmas had been bad. Waking up from the hospital with one lung, a lost baby, and a hideous scar had pretty much set the tone for the rest of the year. I was hooked up to an oxygen tank for about six months after getting discharged. It was a loud machine that beeped and called unwanted attention, so I found myself hiding in my room a lot while I was on it.

When Christmas Eve came around last year, my parents threw a Christmas party. I was hooked up to my machine when my dad pulled me aside and suggested that I might be more comfortable in my room that night. According to him, he didn't want me to grow uncomfortable under the stares of his party guests. It wasn't hard to see that my father didn't want the beeping and whirring of my oxygen machine reminding his *Beauvais* friends about the year our family had. It was fucked up, but I'd somehow convinced myself that I deserved it.

I sat in my room that night and told myself that next year, Christmas wouldn't be so depressing.

I was wrong. It was more depressing.

There's just something about knowing that your parents were ready to bury you that makes you look at them differently.

There was no Christmas party with *Beauvais* guests this year. With Dad running for governor, he was trying to slowly separate himself a little from the elite social club. Dad was trying to come off more "of the people" by staying away from things that might make him look *too* rich. Christmas this year was more of a family affair, but I was kind of out of it. I had a lot on my mind. Later that night, I would be meeting up with Kain so that he could tell me some big dark secret that he'd been withholding for more than a year now.

Even though he didn't say, I felt like it had something to do with my father.

For sixteen months, life with my father had just felt... off. At first I thought it was because of my relationship with Kain, and the implications that came with it. I expected Dad to have gotten over it by now, especially now that it was looking like he just might win the Democratic ticket for his governor run. Still, long after Mom seemed to have gotten over my transgressions of the year before, Dad still treated me like some red headed stepchild.

Whatever Kain was going to tell me tonight, part of me felt like it would explain where the strange behavior from Dad was really coming from.

"Do you think you might go to visit Rashad at the hospital tomorrow?" my mother asked me as we ate Christmas dinner as a family.

About three days ago, members of *The Beauvais* country club were devastated to discover that young Rashad Bordeaux had been making his way back to his Overtown condo when he'd gotten caught up in a dangerous situation.

The Overtown community was in the middle of a controversial gentrification project. The poor people of the neighborhood were being pushed out by rising rent rates and rich people like Rashad. Overtown had become the kind of neighborhood where millionaires lived alongside crack fiends. Income disparities like that are just violent robberies waiting to happen.

And that's what everyone said happened to Rashad—a violent robbery brought on by residents of Overtown's past. He'd been beaten within an inch of his life, and according to most, was lucky to be alive. And from what I heard, as he laid bleeding in the streets, it took hours for someone to call him an ambulance. By the time medics arrived, passersby had already emptied his pockets, and even stolen his shoes.

Somehow, I got the feeling that Rashad's attack had not been as random as everyone else was so keen to believe. Even though many people would have been there to see the attack, no one came forward with evidence. Whoever attacked Rashad clearly had the respect of the entire Overtown community, and they were keeping quiet for him.

"Mom, Rashad and I aren't together anymore," I reminded. I'd sent him a break up text message exactly three days before he was attacked. I would not be visiting him in the hospital. "And I think I'm going to be busy tomorrow."

"You should visit him," my father pressed. "Maybe there's still a chance for you two to reconcile."

"There isn't," I replied tersely, looking down at my dinner plate.

Across from me, Morgan bit back a smile, a sign that she was pleased with my decision.

My father was visibly annoyed, but it was Christmas, so he kept his cool, simply asking, "What's going on tomorrow?"

"She has an appointment with Dr. Eloise at three," my mother reminded, which was odd because putting me in therapy was supposed to have been my father's decision.

"Right," he remembered. You could almost hear him rolling his eyes from his tone alone. "How long are you going to keep going to those things?"

"Until I feel better, I guess." I shrugged my shoulders, wondering, "Why? Is it getting too expensive?"

Dad cleared his throat, setting his fork down on his plate with a loud clanging noise. "No, not at all. I just don't see how talking to a stranger, and telling them all our business is supposed to make you feel better."

"Then why did you put me in therapy?" What a weird contradiction of behavior. "Was that an image thing, too? Did you want all your friends and political colleagues to see that you got your troubled daughter a shrink, so that you could make yourself look like a concerned par—"

"Lauren," my mother interrupted before I could finish. "It's Christmas."

She said that like a warning, as if I'd been nothing but trouble all year and tonight was just the one night she wanted some peace and quiet. But I hadn't been trouble this year.

All this time, I'd been on my best behavior.

I got the right grades.

I dated the right boy.

I said as little as possible.

They still weren't satisfied. I was beginning to doubt that they would ever be satisfied. I was their daughter who had the nerve to defy them once upon a time, and even after sixteen months of well-behaved silence, they would never let it go.

I pushed myself out of my seat, announcing to the room, "I'm going out."

"Are you going to Lux's?" my mother called from behind me. One of the caveats of not having many friends is that your parents can automatically narrow down the possible places you might go. I wasn't going to Lux's, but if I told them that, the alarm bells would start ringing.

So I simply grabbed my jacket, keys, and left without a word.

Chapter Eighteen

KAIN

She was meeting me here.

I'd only just arrived at my apartment from Sanaa's five minutes earlier, peeling off the shirt I'd been wearing all day so I could get a quick shower in. Lauren had sent me a text message saying she was on her way. Her folks lived in Coconut Grove, so her drive up to my Downtown apartment was going to allow me at least twenty minutes alone.

Just before I got in the shower, my phone vibrated with a phone call. Thinking it would be Lauren, I stopped to check the screen, only to forward the call and set the phone back down.

It was Vance.

For days, ever since leaving my visit with Silas, I'd been avoiding my uncle's attempts at contacting me. What Silas had told me last Sunday hadn't exactly sent me on a quest for revenge, but it did leave me feeling like I'd been living some sort of lie.

I used to say that when I was kid, before Vance went to prison, he acted like the mother I never asked for. I would go on to get older and assume that came from a place of strong family values, and he was just looking out. But if what Silas had told me was to be believed, then Vance was replacing the mother he allegedly took from me.

After Silas had dropped the ball, it hadn't been my knee jerk reaction to ask any more questions. I didn't actually want an explanation at the time. One shock was enough for one day. So I kept my distance, leaving Sanaa's house just before her Christmas dinner started because I knew Vance would be there.

My uncle likely hadn't noticed my evasiveness until today. You can write off a few missed calls here and there during the week, but once Christmas Day comes and there's still no contact, most people begin to catch on that they're being ignored. That was probably why Vance had called me three times today. Each call had gone unanswered. When I stepped out of the shower, I estimated that I had about three minutes to get dressed before she arrived.

I hadn't spoken to her much this week. There were a few questions here and there—text messages where she would ask me about a dream she had about something I said, and I would confirm if this was something I told her while she was in a coma last summer. It was bittersweet that she unconsciously remembered so much. So many things had been shared with her that summer, and to think that she held onto most of it, that was beautiful. However, not everything said in that hospital room needed to be remembered.

Somewhere in her memories was an unconscious scene of her father leveraging her life to get me to testify against my father. I felt guilty that I couldn't protect her from that. And I felt guilty that she was coming here tonight to get the rest of the truth.

This past year and a half, I let Lauren go because I felt like no matter how much I loved her, I knew she loved her parents more. It was clear now that they couldn't be the support system she needed. The girl I found at my door that night at *Seven* was a testament to that fact. Her parents undoubtedly weren't doing enough for her.

So I would.

Tonight would be the night I confirmed if I was enough.

* * *

Lauren

In the time since I'd been over his place last, Kain had apparently moved from his father's beach home in Pinecrest.

His new place of residence was a shorter drive from my parents' house, a fortieth floor luxury penthouse in a Downtown Miami building called *The Pegasus*. The place was absolutely unreal.

Kain had come down to meet me in the building's lobby, catching me staring in awe of the coal grey interiors of the first floor reception area. The building was decorated for the holidays, of course, a faux black Christmas tree standing at least ten feet tall with real crystal ornaments, placed as a centerpiece of the entry.

It was so damn beautiful.

If I for one second forgot the level of wealth my ex-boyfriend was living in, this served well to remind me. And here I thought Rashad's condo in Overtown was nice. The lobby of *The Pegasus* building alone made Rashad's living situation look like poverty. If this was what the common area looked like, I could only imagine how grand the top-floor penthouse was.

"You okay?" Kain asked as soon as he saw me. I wasn't used to being around people who were so in tune with my facial expressions. As far as Kain was concerned, the argument I'd had with my parents before I arrived here was written all over my face.

"I'm fine." At least, I was trying to be. I pulled a bag out from behind my back. "This is for you by the way."

"I didn't know we were exchangin' gifts." His eyebrows climbed. I'd caught him by surprise. "I didn't get you anything."

"Don't be too excited," I was quick to warn. "I did all my Christmas shopping last minute. Could you wait until I leave before you open it?" My gift certainly was not a *Cartier* Love Bracelet, and I didn't want to witness it if he was unimpressed.

It was a little after eight o'clock in the evening, and I couldn't be sure what time it would be when I left, but right now the night was young. Even still, as we stepped on to an elevator, I wondered if we would have enough time. When we were together, we hadn't just been lovers. We were friends. There was a lot of catching up to do.

I used to be so uncomfortable with silence. It was with Kain that I learned that sometimes silence could be comfortable. Sometimes you could stand in the presence of a person you cared for, and the fact that neither of you spoke could be intimate.

In that elevator, he checked me out, and I checked him out, too, neither of us seeming uneasy under the attentive gaze of the other.

Was he observing the changes in my appearance? The way I'd grown to like my hair pulled back. The way my waist had narrowed and my once chubby, dimpled cheeks sunk. The way the winter weather made my dark brown skin a few shades different. Kain had never known me in the winter. He'd met me in the spring and we parted ways before the fall. He knew the Lauren who loved to be outside, where the sun was.

I wasn't that Lauren anymore.

His eyes brushed over me openly, seemingly getting a thorough look at this New Lauren for the first time. Nothing in his features gave away what he might be thinking. I returned the gesture, trying to keep a steady expression as my eyes traveled up and down the details of his... everything.

His old brush cut fade made the not so dramatic switch to a typical brush cut, his black sideburns kept clean as they transitioned seamlessly into a wonderfully full beard that he kept short. Facial hair had a way of aging Kain in a good way, giving him an outward air of maturity that had always been present in his personality.

Kain had somehow managed to upgrade what was already perfect.

I felt inadequate.

His changes were for the better, while my changes seemed to only emphasize that I had certainly been through some shit. I wondered if he missed the old version of me, looking at me now.

"You don't talk when you're nervous anymore," he noted. We were on the twentieth floor, with twenty more floors to go.

"Who says I'm nervous?"

"I say you're nervous," he chuckled, as if to say, '*I know you like the back of my hand.*'

And in this regard, I guess he did.

I was nervous as hell. "Well then... Yeah, I don't talk when I'm nervous anymore."

He cracked a faint half smile, shaking his head at my admission. The elevator came to a stop, dinging twice before opening to another door. From his back pocket, Kain pulled out a set of keys, nodding me in to the full-floor apartment.

I cautiously stepped inside, doing all I could do to keep my jaw from hitting the floor. The large space, although probably obscenely expensive, was not ostentatious. It was actually kind of minimal. The modern and sleek furnishings against steel grays and white backsplashes gave the penthouse a luxuriously understated theme. *Very Kain*, I found myself thinking about the place.

We stepped further inside, and Kain set his keys and my gift on a white granite kitchen counter, shaking his jacket off before looking over his shoulder at me and catching my wonder-filled eyes. I took in the beauty of the space, awe-stricken. Situated at the fortieth floor, the main living space was mostly walled with floor-to-ceiling windows that offered a priceless view of Downtown Miami, drawing in the shining lights of the Miami skyline and city traffic thirty-nine stories below us. Even though we were in the heart of the city, it was so quiet up here.

"You like it," he guessed, to which I only nodded, unable to find the words to describe my first impression.

"It's so big," I marveled when I finally did speak, estimating that this apartment was likely three times the size of my parents' house.

"I needed the entire floor," Kain informed, ambling over to a stainless steel, doubled-doored refrigerator. After pulling out two bottles of water he explained, "Privacy has been really hard to come by for the last year and a half."

Of course. The *Montgomery vs. The State of Florida* case from last year totally went viral. While it made my father the laughing stock of the law community all over the country, it turned Kain into an overnight celebrity. The handsome pre-law student who took on a Florida state attorney, and not only held his own, but ruined his career.

Like Kain, Dad was also having trouble getting privacy, but Dad welcomed the fame, because any kind of publicity was good publicity for the new sector he was trying to dive into—running for governor. In elections, name recognition is half the battle, and because of Kain, Dad now had lots of it.

I imagined dating an up and coming popstar wasn't helping with the desire for privacy. When I mentioned this, I tried not to sound jealous.

"You read gossip magazines," Kain surmised, offering to take my coat, handing me a bottle of water as I handed him my jacket.

"Sometimes."

"Then you should know that we released a statement."

"It was a weak one," I offered up my opinion, knowing that as soon as the words left my mouth, it sounded like I was jealous. "'*We're like siblings*,' is exactly the kind of thing celebrity couples say when they get caught."

"Oh, you really were checkin' for those stories." This clearly amused him. "We really are like siblings, though."

"You took her to Catfish Carol's," I mumbled.

"Lauren," Kain stressed, reminding me, "You know I don't like seafood. Eden chose the spot 'cause it's her favorite, too. It wasn't some petty attempt at sending you subliminals. Did you take it that way?"

"Kind of," I replied, my voice coming out small. Reaching for the water bottle in front of me, I changed the subject. "So do you live here alone?"

Hearing my unspoken question, he lowered his gaze to meet my eyes before answering, "Most of the time."

I nodded, my face the picture of understanding, as I uncapped the cool bottle in my hand. I couldn't be upset by this, nor was I surprised. After all, I did read the gossip magazines. And it had been sixteen months.

Forcing a cheerful color into my tone, I simply asked, "So what's her name?"

I wondered if I sounded as possessive as I felt.

Kain sidestepped around that question, redirecting the conversation when he asked, "Would you like a tour?"

Now if I asked him again, I would definitely sound possessive. Trying to keep myself in check, I tried to focus on the things he'd said last Monday, when he told me he never stopped loving me. I ran my eyes over his natural expression. Just as I remembered him, Kain was relaxed and comfortable. I tried to match his energy.

"Sure. I'd love a tour," I replied, trying my best to sound unbothered.

Kain set the bottle in his hand down on the white kitchen counter and motioned for me to follow him with a nod. Two paces behind him, my eyes traced the outline of his shoulder blades through his shirt, and my mind offered me the memory of the way I used to hold on to them while he...

"Lauren."

At the sound of Kain's voice, I snatched myself out of my own head. His eyes were amused when he asked, "You good?"

Silently, I nodded.

"Right, so anyway," he started, stretching out a hand. "This is the living room."

I looked out into the modernly furnished living space, taking in the views of the city and smiling at how the central piece in the room was not a TV, but a bookcase.

That's very Kain, I thought to myself.

"And if we move further down this hall, this is the theater room. At the end of that hall there are the extra bedrooms; nothing too exciting. Come on, follow me upstairs."

This place is two stories high?

At the top of the stairs, we stopped at a transparent sliding door, leading out onto the roof. Kain pulled it opened and waited for me to step through the threshold before he came up behind me.

The cold December air nipped at my nose as I took in the breathtaking sight before me. Kain's private roof deck was a large outdoor space, hundreds of feet into the air, overlooking all of Downtown Miami. The sounds of the city noise were faint and far away. The entire space was lit with string lights that hung above my head, giving off a homey yellow glow. Off one end of the deck was a patio furniture set that circled around a fire pit. On the other end was a covered hot tub, a grill, and a few other things one would expect to find in just about every backyard—except on a roof in this case.

"Whoa," I breathed out, my breath showing up in clouds in front of me. Shivering, I wrapped my arms around myself as I turned in circles, trying to take everything in at once. It was serene out here. I couldn't imagine being stressed about anything with all this beauty around you.

"Come on," Kain urged me to follow him back down and into the house. "You're cold."

The first thing Kain did once we were back inside was turn up the thermostat to a temperature that I knew for a fact was way too warm for him, but perfect for me. After living with Kain for practically two months, his preferences were still somewhere in my head. From what I remembered, Kain preferred the temperature to be at a cool sixty-eight, ten degrees lower than my ideal setting. It would take at least three hours for the whole place to warm up to seventy-eight. I wondered if Kain realized that his actions implied that he was anticipating a longer stay.

Maybe he wasn't trying to be subtle at all.

I stared at the seventy-eight on the thermostat and found myself unsure about what touched me the most—the fact that I didn't have to ask, or the fact that Kain still remembered what temperature I preferred *sixteen* months later.

He wants you to stay. I stifled a smile at the realization.

"And that's everything," he announced, ending the tour and pointing an eyebrow my way as if to ask if I had any questions.

I couldn't help my grimace.

"Is that *really* everything?" I questioned.

Kain smiled at the question, a glitter of mischief in his honey brown eyes. "Is something missin'?"

I twisted my mouth up in thought, a contemplative pucker that I pushed out as I wondered if he was playing with me right now.

"Aren't you gonna show me where you sleep?" I asked curiously, trying to not make the question sound suggestive. Kain nodded, seemingly already aware that he'd neglected to show me that part of his apartment. He nodded for me to follow him down a corridor that lead to a double-doored room closed off from the rest of the house.

"This," he opened the doors, "is my room."

* * *

We laid side by side, on top of his sheets, staring up at the ceiling just like we used to do. This had always been my favorite way to talk to Kain, side by side, heads resting against a shared pillow, with the outside world feeling miles away. I turned my head and studied his profile quietly.

Time really had treated him well appearance-wise. Kain had somehow gotten more handsome. I fought the urge to run my fingers along the short black hairs that were trimmed close along his jaw and chin, connecting to his brush cut. I fought the urge to touch him in general.

"So you avoided my question earlier," I brought up our conversation from before. I just know I sounded jealous.

Kain broke into an amused smile, pleased with himself. "I know."

"I know it sounds so hypocritical since I went off and got myself in a whole new relationship—"

"How about we both just... save that conversation for another day?" Kain was not trying to hear me talk about Rashad. Understood.

Still, I had to ask. "Was it you?"

"Was what me?"

"You *know* what."

Kain turned to look me in the eyes, his expression thoughtful. "You know what's funny about gentrification?" he asked randomly. I raised my eyebrows, inviting him to go on. "You got all these yuppies movin' into dangerous neighborhoods 'cause it's cheaper, pricing people who lived there for generations out their homes, and then when some dangerous neighborhood shit happens to them, there's this outrage. Like that shit wasn't happening to poor folks in that same community for decades. But *now* it's a huge issue? If you ask me, gettin' your shit rocked outside your overpriced high-rise in the middle of the hood is practically a welcoming ceremony."

It was an indirect admission.

I wasn't even the slightest bit surprised.

"As he bled out on the street, bystanders cleared his pockets, and someone even stole his shoes."

Very clearly trying not to smile at that new information, Kain asked, "You choked up over it?"

My mind wandered to images of Rashad pressing me into his mattress, forcing all of his weight into my back after ignoring my protests. I shook my head, being honest when I said, "No."

"Good."

We'd gotten very off-topic in the last couple of hours, talking on just about everything except for the conversation I'd come here to have.

I think we were both stalling. Not just stalling to hold off on whatever traumatic secret Kain was keeping from me, but just stalling for time in general. The longer we held off on that talk, the longer we could justify my staying here, beside him. The beads of sweat forming at the top of Kain's forehead told me that at least three hours had gone by; the entire apartment was now a cozy seventy-eight degrees throughout. Perfect for me, way too warm for him.

"You can turn the thermostat down if you're hot."

"I'll do it later," he replied, the slight melancholy quality to his voice indicating he'd do it whenever I decided to leave. It wasn't hard to see that he wasn't looking forward to whenever that would be.

In truth, neither was I.

"Kain, turn down the temperature," I encouraged softly.

He didn't move, explaining, "I don't want you to get cold."

Breathing in a long inhale, I leaned in to the tiny space that separated us, stopping only when I felt the contours of his body pressing against mine. I could feel the natural warmth of his skin radiating through his clothes, close enough to smell the soap on his skin, and hear the gentle lull of his heartbeat. Where would I even find the willpower to go home to my loveless house, when there was so much love right here? "I won't get cold if you hold me."

Chapter Nineteen

Lauren

"Lauren, wake up."

The sound of Kain's voice pulled me out of my night terrors, his hands holding me down by my shoulders to keep me still. In the dark of his bedroom, his eyes looked over me, alarmed. When I sat up against the bed's headboard, his full attention was still on me. Clearing my throat awkwardly, I looked away and pushed at his chest to put some distance between us.

After waking up at the hospital last year, dreams of conversations I'd had in my coma were not the only thing that visited me at night. On the nights where I didn't dream of Kain, nightmares ate away at my peace of mind constantly. Most of the time, it would be a vivid reliving of that awful night in July, when I felt my life slip through my fingers like sand.

I died that day.

Literally.

There was this chunk of time that went blank between the moment I heard the cracking of the gunshot and then waking up sixteen days later, gaunt, scarred, and childless. Clearly, I went to hell. And I relived that night in my nightmares at least once a week for the past sixteen months. Even nestled in the security of Kain's arms, I wasn't safe from these nightmares. Tears pricked at the backs of my eyes.

Kain reached for his bedside table and switched on a light.

"No." I covered my tears, ashamed of them. "Turn off the light."

Instead, he tiredly sat up and pulled the comforter over his shoulders, leaving an opening for me to climb into his arms and under the covers with him. Wiping away at my cheeks, I joined him under the blanket and he quietly wrapped it around us. Sitting between his legs, my back pressed into his chest and Kain leaned forward, resting his chin on my shoulder.

"How often do you have nightmares?" he asked quietly while slipping an arm around my waist, giving me a sense of stability from the firmness of his hold. I could feel him breathing against my back, the rise and fall of his chest on my back unsurprisingly soothing.

"I don't know, not often," I replied quickly. A lie.

"So all the time?" He easily saw straight through it. Resignedly, I sighed, which he took as a confession. "How long?"

"Sixteen months."

"Have they gotten better since they started?"

"No."

"Do you find it difficult to fall asleep after waking up from one?"

I shrugged, feeling defeated when I admitted, "Wine usually helps me get sleepy again."

"Can I get you a glass of wine then?" he offered.

"It's usually a little more than just a glass."

"I see," he understood, his body shifting around me in a slow move off the bed. "Wait here," he instructed against my neck, the warmth of his breath sending goosebumps along the skin it brushed against. "I'll be right back."

He left the blanket wrapped around me. Before we'd fallen asleep, I'd convinced him to turn down the temperature so that he could be comfortable, and now I was freezing. Kain was back into the room in less than a minute. In his hand he held two wine glasses, and in the other, a dark bottle of Cabernet Sauvignon. It was much fancier than the grocery store variety I was accustomed to polishing off in one sitting. This was not the type of wine you drank straight from the bottle while listening to Erykah Badu.

Kain sat at the foot of the bed and poured me a glass first, stopping half an inch below the halfway point. It was a respectable amount of wine—definitely the amount you'd pour for yourself in the company of others. When he poured himself a glass, I noted that it was slightly a little less than mine—making it obvious that he was only pouring himself a glass to forgo the awkwardness of me drinking alone.

The cabernet was a full-bodied flavor—hints of black cherries with the kick of black peppercorns lingering on my tongue after the first sip. The smooth glide down my throat was practically luxurious, relaxing my tense muscles in what I could only refer to as expensive comfort. I stuck my tongue out to catch the stray drop left on my lower lip, my eyes drawing up to Kain, whose eyes on me felt like heat on my skin from a summery day.

Much to my embarrassment, I'd gulped the entire glass in one go. Wordlessly, Kain extended his own glass, offering it up to me without a hint of judgement in his eyes. I reached for it, setting my own glass down on a bedside table before bringing his glass to my lips for a slower drink than the first. The wine was sweeter now that I took the time to savor it. The tingle of the alcohol warmed my blood enough for the coldness of the room to be cast aside.

Maybe this was the sign that I was developing a drinking problem, but I felt better now for having got the drink in my system. I cast a gratified look Kain's way, which he met with a sympathetic smile. Sympathy was one of my least favorite finds in the eyes of other people, but on Kain, it just reminded me that I was loved. I didn't hate it. I certainly didn't like it, but I didn't hate it.

The warmth in his gaze gave me a happy dose of nostalgia. Kain always used to look at me with such affection in his eyes. That much hadn't changed.

He looked so handsome tonight.

Maybe it was the alcohol, but as my eyes scanned over him, I couldn't help but fall into flashbacks of me biting down on his lower lip when we used to kiss. The smell of his skin was always so fresh and clean against the tip of my nose the moment our lips would touch. The feel of his hands settling at my ass, grabbing two handfuls with a gentle squeeze as he pushed me further to him and against his hardening—

Involuntarily, my front teeth sunk into my lower lip. Kain inhaled tight, and I remembered that he'd always had a thing for the way I bit my lip. Fueled by the power of two glasses of wine, I leaned into his space, stopping only when I felt my forehead press against his chest. His heart was beating at a relaxed pace. This made me roll my eyes. Even after all this time, my heart beat a mile a minute for his presence. And Kain...

Kain always kept it together.

I tried to change the subject. "I'm going to need about two more before I fall asleep."

He thought about it for maybe a second, before ultimately setting the bottle down, denying me of the drink he apparently didn't think I needed. With the shake of his head, I was already trying to change his mind. Just short of my first words, he said something before I could.

The tenderest warning I'd ever heard.

"Baby..." A one-worded order for me to tread lightly. My already speedy heartbeat stuttered, and I felt a jolt between my legs. I lost my nerve, as well as my voice. Saying nothing else, his hand drew up and settled on my face, running soothing lines along my cheek with his thumb. The way his eyes explored my features, analyzing every detail—it had been so long since I'd felt so visible.

Kain's head sloped forward, eyes holding mine as my forehead met his. I closed my eyes, relishing in the feeling of his hands on me. Slowly, parts of us met one another in a deliberate game of suspense. Forehead to forehead. Nose tip brushing against nose tip, our breathing coalescing into matching speeds, his breath hitting warm against my parted lips.

Kain's lips touched mine softly at first, a cautious first reunion since the last time they were together. And then it was like he couldn't get enough of me—drawing back for what might've been a split second before coming back with a force that could only be described as *hunger*. It was like he'd held off from kissing me for as long as he did because he saw this loss of control coming.

With his hands at my waist, he pulled forward, drawing me closer as our mouths joined in a long memorized dance of leading then following, and then leading again. Easily, he pushed past my parted lips, inviting himself in to taste the remnants of the cabernet he hadn't bothered to drink himself. Kain pulled me in as close as we could get with clothes on—chest to chest, lips to lips, tongue to tongue—his hands at my waist traveling downward and stopping at the hem of my shirt.

My breathing hitched, a hot iron of fear searing into my chest at the realization that, with the lights on, I wasn't going to be able to hide it from him. My breathing sped up, but my hands remained still, unwilling to stop him as he drew the white fabric of my top over my head. Kain would see the scar that was permanently etched into me, the ugliest addition to the body he used to know. And even though I knew it would absolutely destroy me if he was disgusted by it, I let him undress me.

His fingers came up behind me, settling at the clasp of my bra. He didn't ask; he didn't even hesitate.

With a twist of his hand, the clasp of my bra was undone, freeing my breasts between us in a move that just screamed ownership. Kain's movements were that of a man who knew I was his; the behavior of a man who knew I would always be his.

He drew back, scanning my half naked body with more than just interest, an appreciative glint in his gaze. I felt beautiful for the first time in a while, but I held my breath as I waited for his eyes to dip lower and see the raised, black gash that was permanently carved into me now. I waited for him to see that I was ugly now.

When his eyes brushed along the dark scar carved into the curve of my ribcage, in true Kain fashion, he maintained his expression, offering no reaction to it. I didn't know if I loved his poker face then, or if I hated it. I both didn't want to know what he thought about it and wanted desperately to know if he thought I was ugly now. It wasn't until the first tear rolled down my cheek that I noticed the saddened prickliness of needles behind my eyes.

Kain didn't immediately react to my crying either. Instead, he reached into the distance between us, taking my head into the palm of his hand and drawing me in closer until our lips met softly. His touch was gentle yet somehow effective in communicating what he didn't say.

You're beautiful, his lips on mine silently announced, before maneuvering away and tracing along the trail the tears I'd shed, kissing them away. His other hand fell to my naked waist, his thumb resting naturally over the raised skin of my scar; nothing in his actions indicating that he was avoiding touching it, nothing in his actions indicating that he was disgusted by it.

Kain touched me like no time had passed between us, like he still remembered my special spots and buttons, like a map of my body was burned into the skin of his mind. I wondered if he still loved me the way he did before. Raising a hand to his cheek, I guided his lips back to mine, feeling a little emotional over how perfectly he fit. My lips over his, his lips over mine, both of us taking turns being the kisser and the one being kissed, a silent conversation between the both of us in the quiet of that room.

I missed you.
I thought about you every day.
I love you.
I love you.
I love you.

In the midst of our wordless conversation, my fingers crept under the cotton of his shirt, the pearl between my legs humming at the firmness of his body under his clothes. By touch alone, I knew the hills and valleys of his muscular form had been well-maintained in my absence. Even after all this time, the image of his body in its full glory was still fresh in my memory. Perhaps I'd held onto it as best as I could, for fear I might never see it again.

I could remember the definition of the muscles along his abdomen, jutting out to meet the curves of my own body under the sheets of whatever bed we'd found ourselves in that summer. I could remember the decorative geometric tattoo on his left pectoral muscle, how I remembered tracing my fingers along its prettiness as we laid together some nights. I remembered every hair, every spot, and every birthmark.

I could remember taking him into my hands, feeling him get harder and watching him grow. It was with enamored awe that I would admire his beauty, both my mouth and kitty watering, my body hungry to get him inside of me somehow.

I was always such an excited giver with Kain.

Coming back into the moment, breathed a sigh of relief over the fact that I didn't have to hold onto the memories so desperately anymore. I had the real man right here, pressed against the palms of my hands. It was with renewed urgency that I felt the need to see him the way I remembered him once again.

My hands gripped at the hem of his shirt, pulling it over his head in a momentary halt of our kisses. In an instant, my arms were around him, pulling him to me in a need to feel his skin against mine. The warmth of his body greeted me like an old friend, holding me so tight you'd think he was trying to prove to himself that this was all real.

"Did you dream about me, too?" I whispered, finding the front of his jeans under my hand, dragging the zipper down with deliberate leisure.

"All the time," he breathed, pulling his head back and analyzing the details of my face. I didn't have to wonder if he found me pretty. Though his eyes were investigative, I didn't feel uncomfortable. Kain always looked at me like I was the most beautiful thing he'd ever seen. Even now. I could remember why it was difficult to feel insecure under his piercing gaze.

I leaned into the distance between us, closing it with a touch of my lips to his. When he parted my lips, I readily welcomed him inside, eager to taste him on my tongue, hungry for the warmth of his passion to caress me in ways only he seemed to know how.

My fingertips at the waistband of his pants pulled down, dragging down his boxer briefs with them, before taking his hardness into my hands. I loved the way his body responded to my touch, feeling him grow rigid against my palm, sensing his body tense ever so slightly at the first initial touch before relaxing again. I loved the sounds he made against my lips as my hand ran up and down the length of his hard flesh, the way it twitched in my hand, the way his breathing changed just a little. When Kain was turned on, he took deeper breaths, tickling the tiny hairs on my skin with each of his equally long exhales.

Damn, when was the last time I thought the way a man breathed was sexy?

It was with this thought that I realized the close attention I paid to Kain's body, his responses, his everything in that moment—it was the same for him and my body. We knew each other's bodies with ease, a roadmap we'd taught ourselves a year and a half ago, and still remembered as if it were yesterday.

Half-smiling, I inched down from his lips, leaving a trail of kisses along his neck and down his chest before ultimately coming down to the throbbing erection I held in my hand. When it came to Kain, I used to love giving head. I think I might've done it almost every other day the summer I tried it for the first time. The feeling of having complete control of his body as he remained at the mercy of my mouth would forever be a turn on.

My tongue slipped out and circled around the head of his length twice before my head dipped lower so I could take a little over half of him into my mouth before he hit the back of my throat.

It was with measured concentration that I slowly took the rest of him down the length of my throat, inch by inch, slow at first to keep my gag reflex at bay. In the sixteen months I'd spent having bad sex with intentionally bad replacements, I could at least find benefit in the fact that I'd learned a few things.

I highly doubted that Kain was the type to feel insecure over the appearance of new skills. When my chin met the skin of his scrotum, I knew I'd taken all of him in. I also would've known from the way his voice turned gravelly when he swore a singular, "*Shit*," under his breath.

The taste of his flesh along my tongue was like an aphrodisiac, getting me riled up enough to stick my hand down my underwear to meet my throbbing clit as my head came up for its first ascension. With my fingers circling feverishly around the nub of my sex, I brought my head down a little slower, repeating the process before my cautious speeds were cast away and I developed a rapid bobbing rhythm. My hand in my panties matched the momentum of my bobbing head, taking all of him in and then three-quarters of him out before coming back down again in repetition, working the muscles of my throat to massage the veiny brown skin of his appendage.

Careful not to bite down, I lightly teased with my teeth grazing the skin of his sensitive head, tasting a hint of precum on my tongue before taking him all in again. His groans and breathless encouragements weren't enough for me. I wanted to make him yell, shout, maybe even scream. I wanted to make him go temporarily insane. My hand slipped out of my underwear, my fingers slick and moist when I took his balls into my palm, eliciting a marginally louder reaction out of him I noted with a full-mouthed smirk. My hand wasn't out of my underwear for thirty seconds before Kain replaced my now busy hand with his own, obviously knowing just the right places to touch me between my thighs. The expertise of his hands was both euphoric and annoying, in the way that he made me quiver into the edge of an orgasm with his fingers alone.

I moaned, a vibration of sound that stimulated the sensitive skin of his penis enough to have him moaning with me. What a beautiful sound it was, lost in a cloud of pleasure, no holds barred. Just free. This was the sign I needed to know that he was close. With that, my speed increased exponentially, taking his entire length down with a hungry speed that triggered my gag reflex once or twice, but I didn't slow down. Not until I felt his balls in my hand tense only slightly, and then twitch with each supply of his hot semen hitting the back of my throat, collecting into a miniature pool on my tongue. Kain's hand settled into the back of my head, combing through my hair and holding my mouth to him as he climaxed a seemingly never-ending supply.

He swore again, something disarmed and weakened about the cadence of his voice, something conquered. I rose my head from him, a triumphant smile crossing into my features as I met his eyes. Kain was breathing like he'd just run a marathon, eyes on me like I turned out to be the opponent he'd underestimated. And I suppose, in some ways, I was. When I gulped down the warm seed he'd emptied out into my mouth, I could've sworn I saw his dick coming alive all over again.

"Lauren," he said between breaths, tone in amused disbelief when he asked, "*How the fuck?*"

He didn't ask when I'd learned to do it *like that*, didn't asked where, didn't ask with who. I don't actually think he cared. It was sixteen months without one another. Of course there would be other people. One day I would tell him about mine, and he would tell me about his, but in the meantime, the only question he had for me was clearly rhetorical.

I shrugged, unable to hold back my smile. It was my turn to poke fun for a change. "I really did that, huh? You need a minute to catch your breath?"

"Funny," he replied, his hand circling around to the back of my head and pulling me in closer. It was me who closed the rest of the space between us, pressing my ear to his chest, breathing out a sigh to the noticeably sped up rhythm of his heart, following his body down as he laid against the pillows of his bed. Just like old times, I brought up a hand to his chest, tracing the permanent ink etched into the skin of his left pectoral, moving my finger along the lines and curves of the beautifully intricate design.

I propped myself up on an elbow, pulling back a little to get a full view of his beautiful form. My eyes traveled down his naked torso, brushing past his reviving penis, down his thighs and then—*wait*.

My eyes snapped back to Kain's naked torso, stopping on something new that hadn't been saved in my memory. In the process of comparing parts of Kain to the image of him I'd saved in my head, I'd completely overlooked the newest addition to his body. A little below the geometric tattoo on his left pectoral muscle, a new line of ink curved along where his ribcage would be seen if not for his muscle mass. The tattoo was dark, the way they tended to be when they were less than a couple years old, displaying the broad lettering of Roman numerals.

VII.XXXI.MMXVI

It was a date, an all too familiar one.

Feeling a lump in my throat forming, I looked down at my surgery scar, dark and raised, running along the curve of my ribcage, and then back at the large tattoo permanently etched into Kain's skin.

They were in the same spot—my scar, his tattoo.

VII.XXXI.MMXVI—Roman numerals that spelled out the date July 31st, 2016.

The day I was shot.

"Kain," I whispered into the silence that fell among us. I was in a state of disbelief, pushing past my stupefied state to get the words out. "Is that...?"

As far as I knew, today was the first time that Kain had seen my scar, and yet somehow he had a tattoo on his body in the exact spot that my scar was on mine. I couldn't speak.

Kain sat up from the pillows, love radiating off of him like heat. Meeting his gaze, it dawned on me that it had been so long since I had felt this safe around a man. It had been so long since I'd felt this secure.

"Baby, I was there," he reminded. "In that hospital room, I was there by your bedside through most of it, for two weeks. Every night from ten o'clock at night to eight o'clock in the morning. I used to fall asleep to the sound of your breathing machine, hoping I'd wake up to discover you woke up on your own in the middle of the night."

I brought my hand to my mouth, drawing in a sharp inhale as tears began to pool at the rims of my eyes. Kain reached in and wiped the first tear that fell from my eyes before continuing.

"I was there the morning we lost our baby." There was something so comforting about hearing him use words like "we" and "our". Before I'd lost the baby, I had this irrational fear that Kain would be too angry at me for lying to him. Angry enough to leave me. Clearly, even though I knew him very well that summer, I still had so much to learn. "I'd woken up to the smell of blood that morning. It scared the shit out of me, and the first thing I checked was your stitches."

For the first time in our relationship, I got to raise a hand to wipe a tear that glided down his cheek. There was so much love in that moment.

"The moment I saw the incision, I knew it would leave a scar. And in the months that followed, the image never really left my mind. It wasn't fair, I thought to myself. I knew that every time you looked at yourself you would be reminded of that night, our baby, me. And that's literally torture. You had to suffer with the reminder branded into you, so it was only fair that I live with the same brand."

Evidently, Kain didn't even have to be a witness to it all to know that I was suffering.

One of the worst takeaways from that night in July a year ago, was not the physical scars, but the psychological damage that seemed like it would never heal.

Some days, I could barely stand to look at myself. The permanent reminder of that day carved into my skin was a constant trigger, forever sending me into horrifying flashbacks and devastating memories. I felt unsafe all the time.

Even wrapped around three blankets, tucked into the far side of my bedroom closet some nights, I still felt like death was always around the corner. On the worst days, I remained in a state of constant fear and dread. Post-Traumatic Stress Disorder is what Dr. Eloise diagnosed it as.

Why did Kain feel the need to subject himself to the same torture?

I asked this.

"Because…" he paused, taking a moment to pull me in closer. It was like he was bracing me for impact, like I might crumble under the weight of what he was about to say next. "The bullet that went through you that night, it… it was actually meant for me."

And with those words, it wasn't hard to put the final piece to the puzzle. The realization came painfully quick. Even if there were a million people who wanted to hurt Kain, I could only think of one who he would try to keep secret from me.

Why was Kain so apprehensive about telling me the truth?

Because he was trying to protect me from the literal pain of my heart ripping in two. Which was exactly what I felt when I finally understood.

Chapter Twenty

KAIN

I would not wish my last twelve hours on my worst enemy.

There is nothing more tormenting than feeling like you just have to watch the people you love suffer. I did that in a hospital room for two weeks last year, but even that was nothing compared to the twelve straight hours of just raw, unadulterated pain that I had to watch her go through.

Last night, Lauren cried for seven straight hours.

And there was really nothing I could do aside from remind her that I was with her every step of the way. The promise was useless, however. I felt useless. Because, in truth, whether I was there or not, that didn't change the fact that her father had shot her.

To add insult to injury, Lauren was also perfectly aware that after her father shot her, he didn't feel remorseful enough to at least give her more than two weeks to fight for her life. He shot her, and he had no problem pulling the plug on the one thing keeping her alive.

The last five hours in the twelve-hour hell I resided in that morning, was spent watching her sleep. I didn't even know people could cry in their sleep. When Lauren finally woke up, even though she'd slept, she was still exhausted.

"I have to get dressed," she mumbled to me tiredly, dragging the hood of a hoodie I'd loaned her off her head. "I have an appointment with Dr. Eloise at three."

Since the office had been closed for Christmas the day before, Lauren must've been written in to wherever Dr. Eloise had availability this week. When our therapist asked me if I wanted a replacement appointment some time ago, I'd refused. Lauren appeared to have accepted the offer.

"Do you want me to drive you there?"

She shook her head without energy, rubbing her reddened eyes with a closed hand. Her voice was croaky from all the crying when she quietly asked, "Are you going to be here if I come back?"

I wouldn't dream of making her go back to her parents' house.

"I'll be here," I promised. The things that I had to do today would just have to be done from home. She was showered and dressed in the clothes she'd come in the night before pretty quickly, out the door in a blur.

I checked the time on the oven clock in the kitchen the moment the door had closed behind her, noting that it was nearly three o'clock in the afternoon. Last night had been a long one, starting off better than I could've ever planned and closing off badly. Very, very badly.

When she realized what the truth had been all along, Lauren became inconsolable. It started off with speechlessness, her freezing up in a catatonic state. I think I might've watched her go into a deep state of shock. And then the tears started. Big, fast droplets pouring out from her eyes and nose, almost endless in supply. I don't think she actually fell asleep. It looked like she passed out from the exhaustion of crying for so long.

I didn't sleep.

For hours, I could only watch as she slept, feeling an odd mixture of devastated that she was going through this, but relieved that the burden of hiding the truth was no longer mine to hold.

It sucked.

No person should have to discover that their father is not the person who they thought he was.

Especially not the way Lauren learned.

Even though I was tired, I couldn't go to sleep. She'd be back in about an hour or so, and I had to be awake to let her in. So I made my way to the kitchen, grabbing a mug from the cabinet and made myself a cup of coffee. When I sat at the counter, my eyes fell on the gift bag Lauren had brought with her the night before. She told me to open it when she left.

The irony wasn't lost on me that the last time I opened a package from Lauren over coffee, I found a restraining order. That was surely nulled now.

Reaching for the bag, I couldn't help but smile when I pulled out a baseball cap. The gift was simple, something most people would just assume I wouldn't be impressed by, but of course Lauren didn't let that stop her. The hat was navy blue, with a capital letter Y in white on the front. On the tag attached, in her neat handwriting was a note.

Because I just know you got in!

I didn't have much time to appreciate it, much less try it on, because as soon as I was done reading the short sentence, a knock sounded from my door. The oven clock said exactly twenty minutes had passed. I figured Lauren had changed her mind about going to her appointment, getting up to go open the door. It was atypical of me to have not checked the peephole. I was tired, though, so it slipped my mind.

When the door opened wide, much to my dismay, my uncle Vance was on the other end.

* * *

"I talked to Silas."

This was the first thing he said to me after he walked passed me and into my apartment. After the night I had, I wasn't really trying to have a back and forth with Vance about my long dead mother, and his involvement in said death. There was no uncontrollable rage brewing from within me over the alleged information. I just didn't take kindly to feeling like I'd been living a lie my entire life.

"Vance, I'm not really tryna have this conversation today."

"What conversation?" he questioned, genuinely not knowing. "All I know is that you went to visit Silas days ago, and you've been givin' me the run around ever since."

"I thought you said you talked to Silas."

Vance nodded, walking even further into my house like he'd been invited in. I felt a wave of irritation fall over me. Persistence was a characteristic in Vance that I often found in myself. But *damn*, it could be annoying.

"I did talk to Silas," he confirmed. "Called him up for Christmas yesterday, and he asked me if I spoke to you yet, like there was something we needed to talk about. And I'm tryna figure out what that is."

"I had a long night," I dismissed, motioning toward the door which I still held open.

Vance squinted at my disrespect, making no moves toward the door. For a moment he just looked at me like he was trying to figure me out, neck pushing out backwards when he dubiously asked, "Silas told you?"

"Yeah." I nodded, pinching the skin between my eyes as my patience wore thin. "He told me."

Vance didn't even look at the door. He doubled down on his decision to stay without invitation. "Then we need to talk about this, Youngblood."

"What's there to talk about? What's done is done. I'll ask you about it some other time."

"No, you will ask me about it *right* now," he demanded, seeming to forget I was not eight years old anymore. I'd never had the desire to lay hands on Vance, but if he kept talking to me like that, that could change real quick. He seemed to be most surprised at the fact that Silas had revealed the truth to me, asking again, "Silas *really* told you?"

I don't answer the same question twice.

"And you really have no questions? You don't want to know why?" This nigga was really trying to have a whole heart to heart about his reasons for killing my mother.

"If it'll get you out my house faster, then go ahead, tell me why."

"It was one of the worst decisions I ever made."

"I can imagine," I scoffed.

"I tried to make it right by being more involved in your life afterwards, but—"

"I don't know why you think I wanna hear this," I cut him off, patience on empty. "Vance, it's really nothing you can say that's about to make me understand your motivations for killin' my mother. Regardless of the backstory, I—"

"*What?*" He posed the question as if what I just said came way out of left field. The way his eyes squinted in confusion at my words was just enough to let me know that me and Vance were talking about two different things the entire time. His second question was equally confused. "Your *mother*?"

Now I was confused, finally letting the opened door go. It shut behind me as I stepped in further. "What are we talking about right now?"

"That's a good fuckin' question," Vance acknowledged, something outraged about him now. "What did Silas *tell* you when you visited?"

I told him.

Vance's expression blanked, before becoming somewhat bewildered.

"Wow," was all he said at first. "He said I killed her? Huh. Nah... Nah, nah, nah, Youngblood. Your mom... We *both* killed her."

Was that supposed to make it all better?

Vance continued, "And Silas chose to leave that part out the story 'cause he knew once the whole story got told, the big bad secret would finally get out. I should've known better than to think he would've actually told you."

"Told me what?" I pressed, hating the fact that it felt like there was a huge chunk of this conversation that was missing. If somebody didn't start giving me some answers...

Vance pushed out a breath, looking me square in the eyes when he revealed, "You ain't his," and then struggled to get the next five words out. "Silas is not your father."

The revelation silenced me.

Those five words slammed into my world almost violently, confirming a question I'd always asked in my heart, but never with my mouth. When you move through adolescence with the blaring reality that your father is the way he is, when you are the way you are, the question does come up one or two times. You push it down, ignore it, because for it to be a valid thing to ask, you would have to question just about everything else, too.

And some questions are better left as that—just questions.

Vance pushed out a sigh and shook his head, his eyes glued to the ball of two hands he rubbed together nervously in front of himself. Again, he repeated, "He's not your father."

I'm not stupid.

When a grown ass man tells you something like that in that tone of voice, he's confessing something about himself as well. Vance laid this new information at my feet as though they were confessions, and that's because—for him—they were confessions. I didn't say anything. In truth, I had no words to give.

Vance continued to unleash.

"I was nineteen years old. She was nineteen, too. Her name was Kiana, and she was..." Vance paused, something that looked like pain flashing in his eyes, "*perfect*."

I was in a daze. This had to be a vivid dream. A nightmare.

"She came from this bougie-ass family up in Memphis, but she was having a bit of a rebellious streak—

trying to get out from under the watchful eye of her pastor father. Yeah... she was a pastor's kid. Her father lead the church that your grandmother went to for years. Her parents were strict

"It was October. Silas was having this costume party for Halloween at one of his old clubs in Memphis and she walked in... dressed as the devil, of all things. Silas took one look at her and marked his territory. She was his before he even talked to her, just because he wanted her. But while he was watching her, she was watching me.

"Kiana was young, immature—naïve at times—in some ways. Not too different from your Lauren, oddly enough. There's this age old saying that men marry women who are just like their mothers. You never even met yours, and yet... Let's just say I'm inclined to believe that saying now.

"Your mother liked me, but she *loved* the attention of being Silas' girl. So she tried to have both, and I, being the young dumbass that I was, didn't care so long as I still got to fuck. There was no feelings attached— not at first. And when she got pregnant by November, I grappled with the knowledge that the baby inside her might've been mine, but I was nineteen... So I took a step back, most of me hoping it would be Silas' kid.

"The months went by and Kiana got more and more pregnant, so of course Silas started cheating. After the first couple of black eyes, she learned to stop complaining about it. She was four months along—it was March—when I was over the house in Miami for Spring Break. I wasn't thinking about Kiana at this point, but we bumped shoulders once or twice during my stay.

"Towards the end of the break, she pulled me aside one day, and told me that the baby inside her was definitely mine. For her own sake, she asked that I keep it a secret. Honestly, I did as she asked for both her sake *and* mine. We had this long ass conversation about how she regretted so much, about how she wished she could go back home to Memphis, about how she missed her parents.

"Kiana wanted to be regular again. She wanted her baby to be regular. For the first time since I'd met her, she was vulnerable—she let me see the real her. And that was the most beautiful I'd ever seen her. I didn't go back to school after that Spring Break. I stayed behind to keep watch over her. Silas' house is a dangerous place for any woman to be, so I refused to leave her there alone. In five short months, I fell in love with her. I would've killed for her. Without hesitation. Much like the way you did last summer for yours.

"It was a bright July afternoon when her water broke—about two weeks before she was due. Silas was out of town, so I took her to the hospital. I held her hand as she pushed. She passed out from the pain, and so I was the first to hold you. I looked at you, and it didn't take much for me to know. I didn't need a DNA test to tell me what I felt in my bones. People would go on to say you looked like Silas, but... so do I. You see my point? When Kiana finally did wake up, she fell in love with you instantly. She named you Tariq, and never let you out of her sight.

"We had a great two months, just living as three. When Silas finally did come around to coming back to

Miami, he took one look at you and knew. Whatever it was that made me feel it in my bones that you were mine the moment I saw you... Silas must've felt the opposite of that feeling. Despite the resemblance, he knew automatically that you weren't his. It didn't take long for him to figure it out, and he was angry with me... but Kiana... he was beyond angry with her. In a fit of anger, Silas pulled his gun out of his waistband, and pointed it at her, telling her she fucked up. I had to think fast and there was a struggle for the gun.

"When I felt it in my grasp, I put my finger through the trigger. Silas' knee drew up and slammed into my stomach, and out of reflex, I pulled. A single shot rang through the air, and the only sound we heard after that was the sound of her body hitting the floor. Silas would go on to swear that he had no intention of actually killing her, claiming he'd just wanted to teach her a lesson by scaring her."

Vance shook his head at the memory. My skin grew clammy.

"I don't know if that's true. I guess I'll never really know. In hindsight, we were both to blame. But at that time, the possibility that it was actually my fault she was dead... I shut down. For months, I couldn't even look at you. I ultimately left, re-enrolling myself back in school as a means to just forget. This went on for years. I buried myself into my school work and tried my best to never have to come home for any reason. Silas never told anyone you were mine—it was a source of embarrassment for him.

"Kiana's death went cold. And Silas changed your name to Kain and had some other woman claim you, so that investigators wouldn't come around asking questions. He said the new name was to honor your late mother, but that was bullshit. Silas changed your name to fuck with me, naming you after a goddamn biblical representation of brotherly betrayal.

"By the time you were three, you'd grown on him. I was graduating from college when I realized he really saw you as his son. After four daughters, God knows he wanted one. It didn't bother me. Why? Because *I didn't want you*. You reminded me of her. You... You have her eyes. Every time I looked at you, I had flashbacks of her lifeless body on the dining room floor, gunshot to her head. So I let him have you.

"And then in my last year of law school, I was interning at a firm in Miami, so I was around a little more often. It didn't bother me to hear you call Silas *'Dad'*. At the time, he was more of a father to you than I ever chose to be. You called me Uncle Vance, we had our times, and I felt like I could live with that.

"But one morning—you were six years old, I think—you and your friend Marlon were in the backyard playing a game where you were pretending to be Silas and he was pretending to be some gang member or something. For six years old, you had such a foul-ass mouth, talking about how when you grew up you were going to be even scarier than Silas."

Vance pinched the skin between his eyes, evidently still infuriated by the memory. I remembered that day as well. It was the memory I shared with Lauren the night I finally let my guard down.

"I snapped," Vance revealed. "Two reasons— one, if your mother could have heard that, it would have broken her heart. And two, because I had an epiphany in that moment—you are *my* son. And I was letting my brother ruin you because I was too indifferent to raise you. So from that moment—that's what I started to do. I raised you. For two years, I did my best to be an involved father. You never missed a homework assignment. Nobody taught you how to tie your shoes, so I taught you. With me, you had chores and responsibilities, you said please and thank you, and you learned right from wrong. All that and then some. Silas quietly took a step back, and didn't get in my way. You were really mine, after all. I knew he hated the reminder, but he stood down.

"And then one night we were coming back from some party—I don't remember. What I do remember was that Silas was driving, and I was not. We'd ended up hitting a group of white girls, and just before the police came, Silas turned to me and said, '*I can't go down for this, Vance.*' I was just short of telling him to go fuck himself, when he simply said, '*But what about Kain?*' and I understood then that he was using you to threaten me. To this day, I don't know what Silas wanted more—to stay out of prison, or to keep me away from you. He got both, though."

My eyes narrowed, and for what felt like hours, I could only stare at my unc—

I swallowed hard, my feet taking a single step backward. The distance between Vance and I continued to grow as no words were exchanged. I had nothing to say to this man. Even as he said his peace as though he had all the reason in the world to make the decisions he chose to make, I lost a significant amount of respect for Vance that day.

Lauren was the love of my life—I understood love perfectly.

I understood how runaway emotions could influence brash decisions, but...

My life as I knew it was a lie. An astronomical lie kept alive by the man standing before me who could do nothing but make excuses and blame broken hearts and love.

I put myself in Vance's shoes. If I lost Lauren in a tragic incident, would I allow my grief to make me abandon our child?

Would he or she look like her? If so, would I find it unbearable to raise a child who was a constant reminder of the love I lost? Could I ever use that to justify saying to that child, 'I don't want you.'?

No.

The answer was no.

Actually, the answer was *fuck* no. Especially if the alternative was giving my baby away to someone like Silas. Why was Vance talking to me as if he wanted me to understand? Who the hell could understand a choice like this? Was there sense being made that I simply could not see?

No...

No—what Vance did was fucked up. I couldn't imagine abandoning my own. Not for healing, not for convenience—not for anything. I often thought about the child Lauren and I lost that summer. He or she would've been almost one year old right now.

The image in my head was that of a baby girl who was an equal distribution of her mother and I. Had she ever gotten a chance to come into this world, I would've celebrated her. In my head, she had her mother's big, dark eyes and dimples, but got just about everything else from me. I had a clear picture of her in my mind as if I'd already seen her, an image so vivid that I'd given her a name.

I mourned her even considering that by the time I found out about her, she was already gone. I loved a child I never even got to see. There wasn't a doubt in my mind that if Lauren had died that summer, and our baby had somehow survived, that I would've loved that child no matter how much he or she looked like their mother.

And yet, for Vance, it was all too easy to leave me behind. Despite how I felt about Silas, I wasn't happy to learn Vance was my father. All the comradery and respect I had for this man was cast aside now that my memories of him were paired with this new information.

The whole time.

He knew I was his son the whole time.

When I finally did find my voice again, it was to offer up a non-negotiable warning. "You need to get the fuck up outta my house."

Chapter Twenty-One

Lauren

"Parents will really mess you up," I whispered into the pin drop silence of Dr. Eloise's office.

My eyes were dry. I think the fluid my body reserved for things like tears was all used up. I knew I looked like hell, dressed in last night's clothes, running on way less than the eight hours of sleep that I needed.

I couldn't tell Dr. Eloise everything. As a health professional, she was required to report evidence to crime. Telling the authorities that Florida's leading gubernatorial candidate was the actual shooter in the shooting of his own daughter... Well, that would certainly get my father charged with multiple crimes—conspiracy, aggravated assault, tampering with evidence, and a slew of other misgivings I was probably not aware of.

Family is a very interesting concept. Only a family member can be hated and loved at the same time so effectively. It was that weird mixture of emotion that made me keep my mouth shut. The man had shot me, and I didn't even want to see him get the punishment he deserved for it. So I didn't tell my therapist the whole truth.

"I'm going to cut off my parents," I announced. "Mom and Dad. Both. I don't think it's healthy for me to live my life feeling like they don't love me the way they should. There's this idea that a lot of people have about parents, that just because they brought you into the world, they have your best interest at heart."

"Parents can be selfish," Dr. Eloise pointed out. "Thousands of children get abandoned every day. Blood is not always the thickest. Just because someone has a child, doesn't mean they will rise to the occasion."

"You're right."

"Can you relate?"

I shook my head. "No. I can't relate. I still think about the baby I should have had. Last summer, when my period was late, I panicked, but I never thought of him as a burden. My mistakes were my mistakes, but I would have never made my child feel like one. I loved him instantly, and I could never imagine choosing myself over him."

Dr. Eloise offered a faint smile. "You envisioned a baby boy."

"I had this baby picture of Kain last summer. His sister had given it to me. It was just about the cutest thing you'd ever seen. And I just…" My voice gave out, and I drew in a steadying breath. "Yeah, I envisioned a baby boy."

"These kinds of family issues happen in cycles. Parents neglect children who go on to neglect their own children until entire bloodlines of loveless family units are made. It only takes one person to end the cycle," Dr. Eloise stated.

"No," I shook my head, correcting her. "It actually takes two. I think your first big decision as a parent, is choosing who the other parent will be. Will that person love your child the way they need to be loved? Will that person be patient? Will they be forgiving? It's all very important."

"And do you feel like that person is Rashad?"

"Rashad isn't relevant anymore," I answered, noting the way my therapist tried to hide the pleased look on her face. "Sometimes I think about my mom, though. I want her to be blameless in the clusterfuck that is my life. I oftentimes try to paint her as some sort of victim. She's suffering under the same hell we all are in my father's house, I used to tell myself. But then I have to remember... she chose him. She chooses him all the time. And she has no problem choosing him over me. That makes her just as guilty."

"And you'll be different."

"I better be different," I replied adamantly. I finally realized the time, and I geared myself to say goodbye. "This might be my last time seeing you, Dr. Eloise."

"And why's that?"

"Like I said," I started to remind her, "I'm cutting my parents off. I don't think I can afford to keep seeing you without them."

She smiled faintly to herself, shaking her head a little as if something was funny. "Lauren, I'll see you on Monday. Same time as always."

* * *

KAIN

"You feeling better?"

She looked better, eyes no longer red and the set of her lips no longer downward. Lauren walked through the doors, a single supermarket bag in her hands along with her purse. From what I could see in the almost translucent white bag, she'd stopped by the store for toiletries, some things to hold her over for the night.

Even though I figured she might, I was glad to confirm she was staying one more day.

"I'm just so angry," she said simply, looking up to meet my eyes. Upon getting a better look at my face, her eyebrows came together questioningly, as if the last couple of hours, while she was gone, were observable on my face. I didn't even have to tell her that Vance had stopped by for her to prompt, "Hey, are you okay?"

I forgot what it was like to be around someone who knew me so well.

"Nah." I shook my head. "I'm angry, too."

Her brows dipped curiously. "What about?"

"It's a long ass story," I warned. She only stared at me, waiting. I nodded for her to follow me to the double doors of my bedroom. "Come on. I'll tell you all about it."

"And before you apologize for that night when you told me Silas killed her—don't," I finished up. I was sitting up on my bed, while she laid down and listened. After telling Lauren about the day I had, I could already see her getting ready to apologize for her hand in this. "If you hadn't told me what you did, when you did, I might've still been in the dark about all of this. Who knows for how long."

Lauren sat up from her laid position, thinking something to herself before she ultimately decided, "Parents will really mess you up."

"Ain't that the fuckin' truth..."

"Are you never going to talk to him or Silas ever again?"

"I don't know," I answered honestly. I had no desire to right now, but never was a really long commitment. Still, I was gonna make the effort. "Probably."'

That was still saying a lot.

We didn't say anything else for a really long stretch. As a form of silent comfort, Lauren laid her head on my shoulder, her hand settling on mine in the dimming light of my room. The sun was beginning to set, washing the room in different shades of orange. The light hit against the exposed skin of her arms, turning gold against her brown complexion. There were no words for how beautiful even the simple things about her were.

From her hands, my eyes followed up the outline her body, showered in the colors of the setting sun, and I slipped my shoulder from underneath her head. I didn't say anything to the questioning look in her eyes, reaching over into her hair, to pull off the tie that held it back.

When her curls fell to her shoulders, Lauren released a sigh.

I loved the sound of her breathing.

The moment I reached for the hem of her shirt, she raised her arms for me. In just her bra and jeans, she leaned in to my space, pressing her lips to mine. When I kissed her back, her arms rose to hook around my neck, moving in closer until she was seated on my lap. Her free hand reached under my shirt, stretching the sleeves through my arms without separating her lips from mine until she was ready to pull the shirt completely off.

My hands rose to her waist, and I felt her tense when she realized my hand rested directly atop her surgery scar. Lauren was very clearly self-conscious about it. Time alone would make her understand that for me, this was nothing. I had her. Scars and all, she was perfect.

I could feel the temperature of her skin rising, growing hot under my hands as the slow work of parting her lips to taste the honeyed flavor of her tongue commenced. The more turned on she became, the faster she breathed, the harder she grinded the heat mounting between her legs against me. From her waist, my hands dropped to the button of her jeans, helping her out of them while she reached for the waistband of my pants.

A small whimper came out of her when my hand passed through her underwear and slipped between her folds, her legs slightly closing around my hand. With the hand I still had, I unlatched the clasp of her bra and tossed it aside. Her nipples poked out hard, grazing along the skin of my chest with the motions of her breathing.

Lauren was wet like I was hard.

Very.

"Mmm," she moaned into my neck, my hands on her ass as I slowly lowered her onto my lap, guiding my dick into her little by little until I'd completely disappeared into her tight core. "Yes," she whispered breathlessly against my skin, her walls clenching hungrily around me. "Kainie—" Hearing that for the first time in what felt like forever drew a soft smile out of me. "—don't cum in me, okay?"

Lauren would say some shit like that to me with the muscles of her pussy literally holding me hostage. Forever my annoying ass tease.

My voice was strained when, against her ear, I replied, "You play too fuckin' much."

The shake of her silent laugh persisted as I lowered her body against the pillows behind her. My body hovered over hers for maybe a single second before I lowered into a kiss, pushing out of her almost completely before bringing it back in hard and fast.

"Ahh." The sound that came out of her might've sounded pained, but I knew her body, and I knew what each sound she made meant. With each thrust into her, her fingernails sunk into the skin of my shoulders, though not nearly as deep as the time I took her virginity.

She was close.

You get to know a person as thoroughly as I got to know her, and you can just tell. So I slowed to a stop, slipping out of her and pulling her waist up and around until her ass was in the air. Lauren waited with baited breath, her breasts pressed against a pillow under her, the arch of her back curving up perfectly to meet my entry.

Her voice was unstable against the force of each inward and outward motion, causing her to stutter out the words she was moaning into the pillows. The muffled sounds of her pleas only somewhat understandable. She was getting to that place where every sentence she spoke ended with my name.

"Yes, Kain."

"Don't stop, Kain."

"I'm close, Kain."

I fuckin' loved all of it. My hands moved under her, taking handfuls of her breasts as she began to throw herself back to meet each of my thrusts. Her hands closed, taking fistfuls of bedding when her body started to spasm under me.

The sounds of her moaning couldn't be contained by the pillow she held between her teeth, the volume of it all bouncing off the walls, announcing that she was climaxing. Water ran down her thighs, the tremors of her body still sending her rocking back and forth along my dick for a little bit longer until she could no longer hold herself up. Lauren was still twitching when I pulled out, heeding her request, and finished on her lower back.

She caught her breath as I reached for the tissues on my bedside table to clean her up. When Lauren finally turned to look at me, catching me admiring the beauty of her body, she smiled, and whispered, "I really missed you."

I couldn't help but laugh at the admission. It was sweet, but I definitely caught the double meaning. What she said was, *I really missed you*. What I heard was, *I haven't been fucked like that in sixteen months*.

"I missed you, too, baby." And she smiled, because she caught the double meaning in my words just the same.

"Kain," she spoke softly when I took my spot beside her. I turned to look at her, motioning for her to go ahead and say whatever it was. She expressed her words like a statement, but she spoke it like a question. "I'm not going back to my parents' house."

And she wasn't talking about tonight.

She was talking about forever.

Chapter Twenty-Two

Lauren

Kain was accepted into Yale a month ago, in November.

He told me this over dinner on his rooftop terrace, three days after I told him I wasn't going back to my parents'. When he told me, I could tell from the caution in his delivery that he'd already decided to go. But he apparently wasn't excited about the decision. I didn't know what he was so downtrodden about.

"It's freakin' YALE!" I shouted, my smile so wide I probably looked crazy. "I knew you would get in! Did you see what I got you for Christmas? Tell me I'm not a pro. You should be excited. They have the best law school in the nation!" Yale had been my father's first choice school before I was born, but he couldn't get in.

"It's in New Haven,"

"Okay, and?" My eyebrows shot up expectantly. "May I repeat, *best* law school in the *naaaaation*." Kain didn't return my smile. "I will break up with you *right now* if you're having second thoughts about *fucking* Yale because you'd rather fool around with me, and… go to Catfish Carol's every night."

He made a face. "Nobody's sayin' no to Yale for catfish."

"So what's with the dull energy?"

"A lot of things are gonna change."

"Yeah." I nodded. "And that's not always a bad thing."

"Not just for me," he explained. "The whole city. Once I leave for good, Silas' whole operation is up for grabs. It'll probably be broken up among several people, and things around here are…really about to change."

"That's not your problem," I told him. "And if you ask me, if the Montgomery name goes on to be associated with the music industry instead of contributing to America's substance abuse problem, then you're on the right side of history. Also, music exec. looks *much* better for your *Beauvais* membership application." Kain's eyebrows dipped with literal disgust. "I'm joking!"

"And I'm gonna miss you," he admitted.

"No you won't," I assured. "You might actually get sick of me. I promise to FaceTime you, and call you, and text you, and when it really gets rough, I can bust out the lingerie and selfie stick. I got you."

The smile that I got out of him wasn't as happy as I would've hoped.

"Come on, Kain, we have to go inside and get your hat. I want to take pictures." I didn't wait for him to shoot the idea down, jumping out of my seat and scurrying into the apartment in search of the gift bag. I could hear his unenthusiastic steps behind me. "Come on, come on."

When I pushed out the hat for him to take, his eyes briefly glanced at my wrist before he took it. He was looking for the bracelet I wasn't wearing. In fact the bracelet was still in its box, hidden in a shoebox in a closet at my parents'. A pang of guilt shot through me, which I tried to mask as I took at least thirty photos.

* * *

"Kain."

We were sitting in his living room, chilling in a comfortable silence, enjoying the presence of one another. He was still wearing his Yale hat, which made me smile. "Yeah, baby?"

"Can you drive to my parents' house with me? I have to return my car since they own it, and get something from my old bedroom." Just one thing. The bracelet he'd given to me for my birthday.

He rose out of his seat, patting his pockets for his keys.

"Let's go."

The drive to my house felt like it somehow got longer. Over the past few days at Kain's, the only member of my family who I'd bothered to contact was Morgan. And even that was only once to tell her to not expect me back. Instead of hounding me for answers and slinging accusations at me, she texted me back a date and time to meet her for coffee so that we could talk about it in person.

I was still on for that coffee date with my twin sister, which was scheduled for tomorrow.

When it came to my parents, however, I had no interest in filling them in to the decisions I was going to make from here on out.

Pulling up to my parents' house was oddly unfamiliar. I'd only been here less than a week ago, but after a few days of being absolutely showered with love and affection, the outside of my childhood home looked like a place I hadn't been to in years. From the cars in the driveway, I could see that both of my parents were home, but my sister was not.

As I killed the engine to the car I was returning, Kain's black Camaro pulled up behind me. I turned to look back at him as I stepped my way up the porch.

His window rolled down, and with a look alone, he asked if I was okay to go in by myself.

With a nod, I stuck my key into the door.

They hadn't changed the locks on me yet.

As always, the inside of my house was quiet. Trying to make as little noise as possible, I didn't bother shutting the front door behind me. The stairs beneath my feet creaked all the way through the slow trek up to my room. When I got there, it looked the same as it always had, filled with memories and personal items that I would've liked to have taken with me. But I was only here for one thing, and I was not about get caught up here because I wanted to take some old toys with me.

Speeding to my closet, I fell to my knees and dug through shoebox after shoebox until I ultimately found the red and gold jewelry box. I breathed a sigh of relief, pressing the box to my chest and making my way out of my bedroom for the last time ever.

Even though I was sure it was all in my head, the stairs seemed to creak under my feet even louder the second time around. I was afraid to even breathe too loud, my eyes falling on the still opened front door as I descended the last couple of steps. I was going to make it out of here without running into anyone. I allowed myself to breathe out a sigh of relief.

Too soon.

"Lauren, what in the hell is wrong with you?" Stepping in from the living room, my father came into view. "Creeping around here and leaving the door all open, had me thinking you were here to rob the place. I could've shot you."

Unblinking, I watched my father tuck a gun into the back waistband of his pants. Beads of sweat bubbled along my hairline, contrasting with the chill I felt run down my spine. I clutched the box at my chest a little possessively, inching closer towards the door. "I was just about to head out."

"What's that you got there? And where've you been?" My father stepped in closer, eyes focused on the red box in my hands. "You been at Lux's place this whole time?"

I neither confirmed or denied the question. Somehow I got the feeling that this was something Morgan might've told him. He was calmer than I expected, somewhat mellowed out. Maybe positive poll numbers had just come out. Maybe it was the Christmas spirit. Either way, I didn't care. There was always calm before the storm.

"Is that box from *Cartier*?" My father squinted at the luxury brand skeptically, his hand coming out to grab the box. I drew it back. He came in more strongly, assuring, "I'm just trying to see," snatching the box away from me.

"Daddy, give it back."

"This must've set Rashad back a boatload. Poor sucker," he chuckled to himself, not remembering that I told him days ago, at dinner, that Rashad and I were no more. Dad opened the box to find the gold bracelet, whistling to himself as he inspected the piece. "I didn't know he could afford this. Is this real gold?"

He brought it closer his eyes, looking for signs it might be fake. I tried to reach for it before he saw, but once he froze, I knew he'd found the inscription.

With love. Always. -K

Dad's eyes snapped up, shooting daggers at me and he let the box fall from his hands. Out went the calm and here came the storm. Like clockwork, every single time. I crouched down in front of him to snatch up the bracelet, fully intending to grab it and make a run for the open door. Dad's palm grabbed at the back of my head, taking a handful of my hair, and pulling me back up to face him.

"I thought you said you weren't seeing that boy."

I felt my eyes begin to water. "Daddy, let go of my hair."

He pulled harder, roughly yanking at my head with every word he shouted next. "WHY. CAN'T. YOU. JUST. STOP?"

The commotion drew my mother out from her office, upon seeing my father with my hair in his balled up hand, the first thing she did was ask him what I did. As if, given the right answer, this could be justified.

"She's still screwing that *boy*!" His grip on my hair strengthened, yanking so rough it felt like he would rip the hair clean out of its follicles. "After everything this family has been though! Just as things were starting to look up! She runs off to be a whore to that lowlife son of a—"

The front door that I'd left open swung wider and Dad stopped talking. Everyone's eyes darted to the door, falling on Kain. Before Kain could take one step closer, my father reached behind him and pulled out his gun, his hand still clutching at my hair.

Dad aimed his gun directly at Kain's head, barking at him to not get any closer. He pulled the safety switch down, staring at the man before us with tunnel vision. Dad seemed to be aiming for the capital Y on the Yale hat that Kain was still wearing.

"Joshua, what are you doing?" my mother spoke up. She was alarmed, horrified. "You're not gonna shoot that boy here, are you?"

Dad didn't even look at her as he responded. Eyes still on Kain, he said through gritted teeth, "He's in my house, on my property."

Kain, as always, didn't even look the slightest bit scared.

Instead, when Kain's gaze met mine in the silence of that room, even though his mouth wasn't smiling, I could've sworn his eyes were.

And I knew exactly why.

Because once upon a time, Kain Montgomery took me to an empty house in the middle of Pembroke Pines, Florida. He pulled a gun out of a kitchen cabinet and walked me to an unfurnished living room. For hours upon hours, he coached me through dozens of situations where I would need to get a weapon out of someone's hand.

That day I can remember sarcastically saying to him, '*You think I'm gonna be able to wrestle a gun out of someone's hands.*'

And he'd confidently replied, '*I know you will.*'

The first thing Kain told me to do when trying to get somebody's gun, was to always push the line of fire out of the way. From there you hurt the shooter enough so that he will loosen his grip, and then when the gun is in your hands, fire until there are no more bullets.

Drawing in a centering breath, I pushed my father's arm up, redirecting the line of fire above Kain's head. Automatically, I drew back a foot, kicking backwards directly at his groin. In response to the blow, he fired a single shot into the ceiling. I brought one arm down slamming my elbow into my father's stomach behind me. His grip on the gun loosened, and with my other hand, I closed my fingers around the barrel and pulled the weapon from my father's hand.

Rather than fire the remaining bullets, I was quick to find the gun's magazine release, pouring out each and every bullet onto the floor. As they watched me take apart the gun, my parents were speechless. I looked over my shoulder to find Kain's smile. His eyes on me were not surprised at what I'd managed to do just now, they were simply proud.

When I turned back to face my father, I looked at the unloaded gun in my hands, and then back at him.

"Daddy." The word came out of me, thick with heartache. "Is this the gun you shot *me* with?"

Fifteen Months Later

Epilogue

KAIN

Weddings are never not boring.

I wish I could say I showed up to my sister's wedding because I loved her.

But that wouldn't be the whole truth.

The house where I'd grown up was an unfamiliar place to me now. It had been almost two years since I'd set foot in the place. I forgot how needlessly big it was. With the way the backyard opened out to a private beach, and the endless amount of room inside, Sanaa felt like it was the perfect place to get married.

I walked the halls of the old place, remembering the bodies in the dining room, the bodies in the living room, the bodies in the kitchen. This place was haunted with more ghosts than I could count. Not a perfect place to get married at all.

But when Sanaa planned an event, she planned an event. My opinions would fall on deaf ears. At least she was smart enough to have the ceremony outside. While guests took their seats in white chairs along the beach outside, the inside of the house was reserved for the chaos that any wedding would guarantee.

"Where THE FUCK are my shoes."

"You told me you were a size SIX! Not my fault you got fat!"

"No you cannot wear a FUCKING waist trainer in that dress!"

"Stop drinking the champagne!"

"If any of you DRUNK BITCHES trips on your walk, I swear TO GOD."

"Has ANYONE seen the FUCKING photographer!"

"Cierra, this is MY day. Stop posting my SHIT all over Instagram!"

I could hear Sanaa shouting throughout the house as the wedding party scrambled to meet her every whim. Blurs of yellow and white going from here to there, rushing to meet the demands of the bride-to-be who was probably going to lose her voice before she got the chance to say her vows.

It was March 3rd, 2019.

The first Sunday in March, and the first Sunday of my week long stay in Miami. I could've thought of about a dozen different ways I could've spent my first day on Spring break.

But I was here because *she* was here.

Not my sister.

Lauren.

A stream of yellow fabric whizzed passed my face and I held out an arm to stop and ask. "Cierra, have you seen—"

"No." Cierra shook her head before I could get the question out. "I haven't seen her."

"Do you know where I might find her?"

Cierra held up her cell phone. "Okay, so there's this really cutting edge technology called the text message. You might want to try it."

Like I hadn't already tried that.

"Thanks," I replied dryly.

"If it helps," Cierra mentioned, "She's wearing a yellow dress."

Cierra thought she was being funny. All of Sanaa's bridesmaids were wearing yellow dresses. And Sanaa had about twenty-five bridesmaids. The wedding had too many guests, and was ridiculously over the top. But that was Sanaa, though. It wouldn't have been normal for the event to be normal.

Sanaa's wedding was the society event of the season. Even the governor was here. Though, that wasn't surprising. A lesser known secret was that Governor Perez wouldn't have won the election if not for the Montgomery family. It wasn't him that I liked. It was his opponent who I hated. So he won. And for that, he owed the family an endless list of favors.

I walked around the entire first floor, checking the face of just about every yellow dress-wearing woman I found. When I stopped in the kitchen, even though I still hadn't found her, I saw flashbacks of her from three years ago, taking shots at the kitchen island, in that red dress. I smiled at the memory, ambling down the halls until ultimately stopping at the staircase.

I thought about it, and figured *just maybe*. So I took the steps up to the second floor, moving down the hall to the last door on the right. It was already slightly ajar when I stepped through the threshold and into my old bedroom.

"BOO!"

I didn't jump. Nor was I startled.

With a smile already forming, I turned to find her coming out from behind the door.

"I didn't even scare you a little?"

"No," I replied, cupping her face between my hands and drawing her in closer. Lauren filled out that dress perfectly, wearing it better than every woman I'd seen in it downstairs. All things considered, it was still ugly as shit, though. "You look like a lemon."

She made a face. "Excuse you. A cute lemon."

"Right," I agreed, pulling her even closer, my lips hovering over hers when I added, "A cute lemon."

She pulled back after the first kiss, making it perfectly clear, "I can't have sex right before the ceremony."

"You can't?" I asked, sounding amazed. I brought Lauren right back. "Says who?"

Lauren tilted her head, giving me wider access to her neck, explaining as I worked, "Your batshit bridezilla sister."

I hadn't seen her since December. I needed her right now. The feel of her skin, the smell of her hair, the way she tasted.

"Sanaa's harmless," I dismissed, still carrying on with my task.

"No, she's not," Lauren assured, laying backwards onto my bed to give me better access. "I'm pretty sure she killed one of us. Only twenty-four bridesmaids showed up."

"Twenty-three," I whispered against her collarbone.

"No, I'm not skipping," she argued. "And tread carefully, if you ruin this dress before the ceremony, Sanaa will kill you."

"That's fine," I assured, then changed my mind. "Wait no, it's best we both make it out of this wedding alive. Take the dress off."

Her hand glided the zipper of her dress down, exposing a sheer lingerie set. Yeah, Lauren knew what time it was long before I found her in this room. She came ready. "Do you know what tomorrow is?" she asked.

"March 4th," I whispered against her lips, slipping a finger underneath the waistband of her underwear. "How do you wanna celebrate?" I asked as I pulled them down her legs.

"I was thinking that maybe we could—mmm," she was cut off by the surprise of me running my tongue between her folds. "Maybe we could have... uhh... date to... date to... We could do this again. This would be... ahh... just perfect."

"At least make me take you somewhere first," I encouraged, immediately going back to her clit. Her hips rocked between my hands, body squirming against my tongue as I tried to keep her still.

"Dinner," she breathed. "Make me... dinner. Like how you did... when we first... started out..."

"And then?" I asked.

"We could do this again."

New Book!

Coming October 2018:

The Garden of Eden

First in a series of romantic standalones, The Garden of Eden opens with R&B princess, Eden Xavier, on the last leg of her first North American tour. On the night of her final show in New Orleans, Louisiana, she meets Andrew "Drew" Lavigne in a case of mistaken identity.

Drew Lavigne is the son of a megachurch pastor, heir to a thousand-member congregation in the heart of New Orleans, he feels like he moves through life with a thousand pairs of eyes on him at all times. The night Eden Xavier, world famous R&B singer climbs into his car, mistaking him for her Uber driver, his world of local scrutiny becomes nationwide attention.

Eden and Drew face different pressures on both sides, and just before they crumble under it, they find each other.

Kain and Lauren are minor characters in this story.

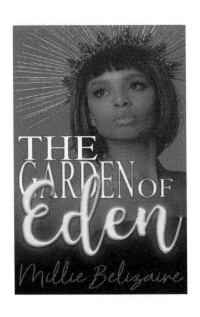

Made in the USA
Columbia, SC
28 November 2024

47788294R00176